Locked in Silence

Praise for Shiloh Walker's
Locked in Silence

"Walker's (*Hunter's Fall*) race of angels are darker and more violent than their namesake tales, and the book contains graphic scenes that veer into power play... Readers who enjoy their romances on the dark side will find this a welcome edition to the series."

~ *Library Journal*

"This is a story filled with edge of your seat action, scorching hot passion, and a couple of heart-rending moments to it... There are a couple of things I recommend with this: tissues and lots of iced drinks."

~ *Long and Short Reviews*

Look for these titles by
Shiloh Walker

Now Available:

Always Yours
Talking with the Dead
Playing for Keeps
For the Love of Jazz
Beautiful Girl
Vicious Vixen
My Lady
The Redeeming
No Longer Mine
A Forever Kind of Love

The Hunters Series
The Huntress
Hunter's Pride
Malachi
Hunter's Edge

Grimm's Circle Series
Candy Houses
No Prince Charming
I Thought It Was You
Crazed Hearts
Tarnished Knight
Locked in Silence

Print Collections
Legends: Hunters and Heroes
The First Book of Grimm
The Second Book of Grimm

Locked in Silence

Shiloh Walker

Samhain Publishing, Ltd.
11821 Mason Montgomery Road, 4B
Cincinnati, OH 45249
www.samhainpublishing.com

Locked in Silence
Copyright © 2012 by Shiloh Walker
Print ISBN: 978-1-60928-707-8
Digital ISBN: 978-1-60928-528-9

Editing by Tera Kleinfelter
Cover by Scott Carpenter

This book is a work of fiction. The names, characters, places, and incidents are products of the writer's imagination or have been used fictitiously and are not to be construed as real. Any resemblance to persons, living or dead, actual events, locale or organizations is entirely coincidental.

All Rights Are Reserved. No part of this book may be used or reproduced in any manner whatsoever without written permission, except in the case of brief quotations embodied in critical articles and reviews.

First Samhain Publishing, Ltd. electronic publication: September 2011
First Samhain Publishing, Ltd. print publication: August 2012

Dedication

For my family, always...

Prologue

"Would you *stop* hovering?"

Will was hard-pressed not to gape at her. He did *not* hover. He brooded, he pissed people off, he did things he hated, things that made others hate *him*, but he did *not* hover.

He'd walked the Earth for more years than he could remember, and he'd seen friends, both mortal and angel, die and he'd taken it all with the knowledge that death was inevitable. He didn't falter in his tasks, he didn't hesitate and he damn well *did not hover*.

Even as that ran through his mind, he kept two steps behind her, worried Mandy might stumble as she made her way to the balcony.

He'd like to think—indeed, he even *told* himself—that he worried over all the newly made Grimm this much. He was their leader and it was his job to watch over them.

It was never an easy thing, that change from mortal to more. And when one went down the way Mandy had, in a bloody, brilliant blaze of pure selflessness...

The images tore through him again, as though it had happened yesterday. In truth, it *was* like yesterday for him. Six months was like a second to him, a blink, a heartbeat. Days blurred together and faded. People blurred together and faded. Even his Grimm, sometimes.

But not Mandy.

She was as vivid to him, as bright and brilliant and bold as a bolt of lightning.

Nothing about her had faded, not in the five years since she'd come into his life so unexpectedly.

She glared at him over her shoulder, dark eyes snapping, her face pale and wan and too thin. She needed to eat more, gain back the weight she'd lost before her body took on the form she'd carry for the rest of her existence.

"You're doing it again," she said, her voice carrying a warning edge.

"I'm not doing anything," Will said stiffly, wondering how he could get her to sit down. To eat. To rest.

It had been four days since he had brought her out of stasis.

Four days…and every time she opened that smart mouth of hers, he was torn between an urge to strangle her and kiss her. Of course, he couldn't give in to either option. And damn it, if she didn't sit down—

She was so thin, so pale. He could almost see through her, it seemed.

She spun around and slammed a hand against his chest. "*Stop* hovering!" she snarled, her eyes flashing at him.

"I'm not hovering," he said.

Mandy lifted a black brow. "And what would *you* call it, Will? You're never more than three feet away, and if I'm standing, you're more like *two* feet away, at the most. Let me breathe, damn it. Let me…"

She swayed and he caught her, steadied her.

"Shit." She smacked at his hands as he lifted her, carried her to one of the chairs out on the balcony. "I hate this. I hate it."

He smoothed her dark hair back from her face. "The weakness will pass. You just need to let your body adjust. You need to rest, eat. Give yourself time."

"How much time? Shit, I've been out of it for six months..."

He knew. He knew in excruciating detail just how long she'd lingered in stasis—he'd spent almost all of that time at her side. Watching. Waiting. Wondering. Worrying.

Regretting.

This woman, somehow, had worked herself so deeply inside him...

The injuries she'd taken upon her death had been so grievous, a few hours, a few days hadn't been enough for her body to heal the damage, Grimm or not. No, it had taken months, and he'd spent those months at her side.

He felt a familiar press on his mind. Sighing, he straightened.

Mandy gave him a puzzled glance then smirked. "Obi Wan Kenobi needs to commune with the Force."

He tuned her voice out as two familiar faces came to his mind.

One of his Grimm.

And a mortal...who was slated to become one of his.

She'd already had such a hard life—

Vanya.

He'd hoped she would have more time. Enjoy her mortal life.

But she hadn't enjoyed the first twenty-three years. Why in the hell should that change now?

Chapter One

"Can you see through my dress?"

Vanya tried not to snort as she finished up in the bathroom stall. When she came out, she automatically dipped her head so her hair—or rather the wig's hair—fell and hid the scars that started at her temple and continued down along the left side of her face.

The wig was a necessity. The scars made her stand out too much. In the past two years, she'd convinced herself not to care so much about them, but the reality was that they did make her stand out and she couldn't have that.

If she didn't do something to disguise her looks, it would be far too easy to track her down. And she still suspected it wasn't enough.

Of course, tonight, it hardly mattered. These girls weren't paying her any attention at all.

They were too busy staring at their friend's dress.

"Oh, you can definitely see through it."

Yeah. Vanya was hard-pressed not to roll her eyes as the girl clapped a hand to her forehead and dramatically cried, "I look like such a *slut*...why didn't anybody tell me?"

"Well, we thought you knew..."

The dress's transparency wasn't going to add or detract from the girl's would-be sluttiness. Maybe the fact that it didn't quite cover her lacy boy shorts, her lack of a bra and her very real need for one—*that* might add to the slut image. Or the fact that she'd already had sex tonight—*twice*. Vanya had seen the girl going at it outside on her way in—and she'd also seen Ms. See-through Dress fucking a different guy in the bathroom here earlier.

Vanya noticed things.

Lots of things—particularly in places like this.

Places like this—rank, nasty dives that made her want to take a bath.

But she needed to be here.

Tonight.

Vanya didn't even know why.

She just knew she needed to be here.

Even though it was screwing with her head something awful. Too much going on—too much sex, too much anger, too much confusion and chaos and depression and sadness and want and lust and greed…

All the thoughts pressed in on her and she couldn't block them all out. It was as if she'd walked into the local Best Buy and somebody had jacked up all the speakers to maximum.

She hated it.

The noise, the chaos, they screwed with her shields something awful.

She did fine one-on-one, two-on-one, even ten- or twenty-on-one. But a few hundred angry, angsty young adults and not-so-young adults who were trying desperately to pretend they were…hell, it was enough to screw with any psychic's shields. At least, she'd prefer to think so.

Locked in Silence

To say her shields were compromised was putting it mildly.

This wasn't a place she *wanted* to be.

And if she listened to her instincts, she'd leave because there was danger in every corner here.

Death waited.

She could feel it, all but taste it.

She hadn't tasted it this strong since the night her sister Irina had died—been killed.

The night Vanya had killed her. Killed her and the demon inside her. At least she'd *hoped* the demon died. She didn't know enough about the demons to know for sure. After all, nobody would tell her. She suspected not many *could*. Those who could weren't talking.

A giggle pierced the dark shroud of Vanya's thoughts and she braced her hands on the cool porcelain of the sink, made herself think. Made herself focus. She needed to get out of here. Back into the club.

Where *they* were.

The succubae and incubae.

The demons.

They were her main concern—the reason she was here.

She didn't need to be worrying about a bunch of giggling, silly girls. Girls who were busy lamenting over a silly, sheer dress and whether or not any of them made a hookup tonight.

Vanya wished that were the biggest concern of her life.

That hadn't ever been a concern in her life.

She rarely had time for it.

No—her biggest concern was currently centered around the demons who had selected this bar as a feeding ground. Even though they were stronger than her, faster than her...

Even though they could kill her with ridiculous ease.

Kill her—

But then again, that was her goal, wasn't it?

She couldn't really make any real progress until she died.

I've got a deal for you...

Like it was yesterday, Vanya could remember the night he'd come to her.

His name was Will. Or at least that was the name he'd given her.

He was one of the people who could enlighten her about demons. But he wasn't too interested in sharing many details with her. At least not yet. *In good time*—that was his favorite line.

One would think he'd be more interested in talking to her, reassuring her. Considering he was trying to convince her to join him. And in order to do that? She had to die. Yeah, that was a real kicker. Some reassurance would be appreciated. But he never gave it, and oddly enough, she trusted him despite that fact.

She'd met him five years ago.

Five years ago—she'd been eighteen and alone, fighting against those things, like she'd been doing as often as she could, ever since she was sixteen when her sister had been taken over by them. Her sister, her friend, her only family.

Then...

"I've got a deal for you."

He'd come out of nowhere. Dressed all in white, from the long, white leather coat, to the white leather shoes. On many men, it would have looked foolish. On him...it fit.

Vanya, covered in blood, still shuddering from the rush of adrenaline, had barely been able to keep the scream trapped behind her lips when the man practically *appeared* right in front of her.

Not that he had—that wasn't possible.

But it sure as hell seemed that way.

With a sneer to cover her fear, she started to go around him. "Sorry, pal. If you're looking to get laid, you're looking in the wrong place."

He caught her arm. "I'm not looking for sex, Vanya. I'm looking for fighters. And that's what you are. An hour of your time, in public, and I'll buy you a meal."

The exact right words—he couldn't have offered her diamonds with a better result.

Her belly growled. It had been more than a day since she'd scavenged up a decent meal. Although she had the money she'd stolen from her latest kill, if this guy was willing to fork over the dough...hooking her thumbs in her pockets, she studied him.

"A meal and fifty bucks," she said, lifting her chin.

He smiled. "Not a problem. Shall we?" He gestured toward the road.

But Vanya hesitated. She'd just killed two...things. They'd been human once and their bodies still looked human. That meant they'd *bled*...a lot.

And the police would think she was insane if she told them some story about demons and possession...

Plus, although the dark clothes she wore hid the blood pretty well, in the light, people would notice something.

"I'll meet you. Someplace. Two hours. I've got a prior engagement," she said.

"Ahhh. Yes. It wouldn't be a bad idea to clean up, change your clothes, I imagine."

The blood drained from her face—she felt it. Swallowing, she stared at his face. And although she didn't like to do it, she lowered her shields, just a bit, prepared to jerk them back up in case he felt like...one of them.

What she felt was...

Weariness. Strength. And light—it was almost like she stood in the sunshine after years and years in darkness.

Hissing out a breath, she backed away, staring at him.

Judging by the look in his eyes, he'd known exactly what she was doing. He continued to watch her, waiting, a patient look on his face, as though he'd wait forever. As though he *could* wait forever.

Suddenly, she wasn't so hungry and she didn't think he was worth the fifty bucks or the free meal.

"Maybe not, but that deal I mentioned? It's worth it," he murmured. "You'll end up dead, one of these nights, when you go out there. You'll continue this quest, determined to kill those things before they take away somebody else's sister, mother, brother, son...but this time, you'll be the one to fall. The one to die. Or perhaps worse—you'll end up one of *them*. It's a risk and you know it. It's a fear you live with. The nightmare that keeps you awake, even though you sleep only during the day when the sun shines bright in the sky."

Terror squeezed her chest, her throat.

Shit.

Shit.

Shit—how in the hell—what the hell—?

"Who in the fuck are you?" she demanded. "How do you know that?"

The smile curling his lips was sad. "Somebody not so different from you, sweeting." He reached inside his pocket.

She grabbed her knife, brandished it.

And then felt very much the fool when he held out a crisp fifty dollar bill. "Yours...whether you meet me or not—the good Lord knows you could use a good meal or two on you. Your favorite restaurant. Be there. In two hours. Or not. But I mean you no harm."

"What do you *want*?" she demanded.

"Meet me...or not. Like I said, I have a deal for you, Vanya. One that will make you faster, stronger...and you'll be able to kill all the monsters you wish. And they'll never be able to take you over. That nightmare, the one that haunts you? You'll be free from it. Forever. I promise you."

He turned around and strode away. She stared at him, dimly thinking she hadn't told him her favorite restaurant.

Free...

She shook her head, trying to make herself listen to common sense, and not that desperate, desperate hope. *He's just a quack,* she told herself. One who hadn't even *asked* her what her favorite place was, so how could he meet her?

"I'll be there, Vanya. I promise. The question is...will *you* be?" he called out over his shoulder.

A quack—a freaking *weird* one.

One who...holy shit.

He'd fucking disappeared.

Right in front of her.

"So...did I pass the test?"

Vanya swallowed as he slid into the booth across from her. Yeah.

He'd passed her very strange test, but she wasn't about to tell him that. In the past one-hundred-and-eighteen minutes, she'd showered, changed her clothes and hit two different restaurants—the first one had been her favorite.

This one had been her sister's favorite.

What she wanted to know was how he knew that, how he knew to be here.

He's following me, that's all, she thought.

"I'm not following you. You were at the roadhouse for a while and left, though I know it was your favorite." He smiled and leaned back. "You were last here with your sister. On her birthday, three weeks before she died. You bought her dinner, spent your entire paycheck on it. It meant a lot to her."

Tears sprang to her eyes.

"How do you know that?"

He glanced around, a casual glance, one that probably nobody else would have noticed.

She wouldn't have thought anything of it, if she hadn't felt a prickle across her skin.

Goose bumps rushed over her skin. She'd felt something...similar. The same, but not, when she was the presence of those things.

Terror rushed through her, and suddenly, she was very, very glad she'd strapped a knife on before she'd left the little, hellacious hotel room where she was currently staying.

"You won't need the knife, Vanya. I'm not going to hurt you," he said quietly. "And I'm not one of the demons."

She licked her lips. "Duh...demons?" Yes, she *knew* they were demons. It was the only thing that made sense, but nobody else seemed to believe her. She'd even tried talking to a priest at a Catholic church, and although he hadn't said it out loud, he'd been convinced she was either on drugs or mentally unbalanced—she'd seen that in his mind. "Demons. You believe in demons, old man?"

Old man—he didn't *look* old. Despite the silvery hair, despite the look in his eyes.

He stared at her, a strange smile on his face. "Don't you? The kind you killed earlier were incubae—male demons who thrive off sexual energy. Their female counterparts are succubae. They seem very drawn to you, and you've got a knack for sensing them out. I think it's because of your sister. There's a strange bond there."

Demons. Incubae—he'd called them a name. And he was talking about them just as causal as can be, right here in the middle of O'Charley's where anybody could hear them.

He grinned. "Nobody can hear us. That's what you felt a moment ago...I was muffling everything. They'll hear the hum of our voices but no actual words. A handy little gift I have."

She blinked. "You're crazy."

"No. Would you like me to prove it? We can be as loud as we want, talk about whatever strange things we wish and nobody will notice."

"Ah..."

"Go ahead, try it out."

The waitress appeared then, smiling at them, that professional, polite smile fixed firmly in place. "What can I get you two?"

"Ah...a Coke," Vanya said, intentionally talking a little louder than necessary...and watching as the waitress's smile wobbled a little. "And the appetizer platter. Make the wings extra spicy." He was buying, crazy or not, she was getting as much food as she could.

"Just ice water for me," the man said, keeping his voice level.

As the waitress walked away, Vanya looked back at her very strange companion and said, "Well, there's the proof I needed. She heard us just fine. And she thinks I'm either a moron or deaf."

"Because we spoke *to* her. Try screaming at me. Nobody will hear." He waited, a brow cocked, a challenging grin on his face.

She hunched her shoulders, glancing around. Shit, she was in the middle of O'Charley's with a lunatic.

He started singing.

Loudly. He had a great voice, she noticed—she didn't know jack about singing voices, but he sounded like he belonged on a stage somewhere, and that deep, mellow voice carried. Although she wasn't *quite* sure that "Henry the Eighth I Am" was going to win him any record deals.

Blushing hotly, she shot a look around. "Would you..."

But nobody was looking.

Not a soul.

He stopped singing. "They can't hear me, Vanya."

"Ahh..." She licked her lips. Feeling very much like an idiot, she screamed. It was a weak, chirping little sound, but definitely loud enough that somebody, like the people behind them should have heard. Nobody so much as peeked at her. "Okay. This is weird."

Shifting her gaze to him, she asked, "What in the hell are you?"

He smiled. "I'm a guardian angel."

Vanya laughed.

He sat there like he'd expected just that response, his silver eyes vacant, that polite smile remaining firmly in place. Something about the way he sat there, so unaffected, killed her amusement very, very fast.

"You really want me to believe that."

"It's the truth," he said, lifting a shoulder in a lazy shrug.

"A guardian angel."

"Yes."

"Bullshit."

He leaned forward and now the look in his eyes wasn't vacant and he was no longer smiling. He wasn't angry, she didn't think, but the look on his face was...intense.

"You believe in demons, Vanya. And don't bother answering that—I already know the answer. I sense it, I feel it. You're psychic and your shields are excellent, especially considering how young you are and the fact that you're untrained. How can you believe in demons...but not angels?"

Staring into his eyes, she decided that was a very, very good question.

She licked her lips, uncertain how to answer. Looking away from that intense gaze, she found herself staring at the little girl at the table across from theirs.

A pretty little fairy, she thought absently.

The girl smiled and waved, showing her a gap-toothed grin. Automatically, she dipped her head, hiding the scars on her face, not smiling back.

"You can smile at her, you know...children don't care about scars the way adults do. Your scars don't bother her. She just wants a smile. She's not afraid of you."

"Like I care," Vanya muttered. But, despite herself, she found herself trying to smile. "I don't even know her."

The little girl's smiled widened and she went back to scribbling on the coloring book in front of her, babbling to her mother.

"If you didn't care, you wouldn't be so worried about scaring her," Will said quietly.

Shame and sadness wrenched her heart and she looked back at him.

He stared at her, his eyes locked on hers. Looking at *her*, not the scars.

They were ugly—three raised, ridged marks running down from her temple, down along her cheek—scars her sister had given her. Right before Vanya had killed her.

In the days following, an infection had settled in, almost killing her. Vanya had been living on the street and it wasn't until she'd collapsed that she'd gotten medical attention. Of course, she'd also almost ended up in foster care, would have, if she hadn't read the nurse's mind and run away only an hour or so before she would have been put into the care of the state.

"I don't like having people read my mind," she said, bolstering her shields as she studied his face.

"I'm not reading your mind. I just...know you. I've been watching you for a while. Keeping an eye on you, making sure you weren't in over your head."

She curled her lip at him. "I can take care of myself."

"Of that, I have no doubt. Which is why I'm here. About that deal..."

Now...

He'd laid out the deal that night.

She'd accepted, still half-thinking he was out of his mind.

Even though, somewhere inside, she knew he wasn't.

Will was about as sane as they came.

And tonight, she realized, it was time for her to make good on that deal he'd offered.

She hadn't thought she'd be so afraid.

Her hands were sweating.

The death she tasted in the air—it was hers.

And they were close.

Succubae, incubae—more of them. Man, she hated their kind. They so loved this sort of place. Hot and ripe for the picking. Full of the young, the restless and the horny.

After that first initial rush, her heart rate settled down to something resembling normal and she leaned closer to the mirror, under the guise of examining her makeup.

The girls were still jabbering. Still giggling about dresses—somebody else's now. Feeling sort of disconnected, Vanya realized they had noticed her. Habit, forged in a lifetime where she'd been happier to fade into the background, had her wanting to hunch her shoulders and mumble an apology, disappear. Instinct dictated she stay where she was.

Pride did the same thing.

Pride also had her lifting her chin and meeting the gazes of the girls in the mirror.

That was when they saw the scars.

Eyes widened.

Mouths dropped.

Over the past few years, Vanya had learned *never* to let anybody see a reaction off her, not through a blush, a nervous smile or laughter. One girl—the girl with the transparent dress—met Vanya's gaze then shifted her stare to the scars.

With a snicker, she jabbed her friend with an elbow and said in a pseudo-whisper, "Geez, hasn't she ever heard of plastic surgery?"

"Holy shit, Robbi, you didn't just say that!" One of the girls, her face stricken, looked at Vanya with wide eyes. "Girl, I am so sorry. She's drunk and she doesn't always think good when she's drunk. I'm sorry."

Turning around, Vanya lifted a brow. "Why? You didn't say it." Then she looked at Robbi, studied her face and wondered if this foolish kid would live through the night, if Vanya would have to be the one to kill her.

It bothered her. Life was precious—Vanya had seen too much death

But whether it bothered her or not, Vanya wouldn't let it stop her. If the girl let one of those things inside her, though, Vanya would kill her. Robbi wasn't strong enough to fight it, and Vanya would be damned if she let the little bimbo infect anybody.

She wasn't precognitive, although she did have a knack for knowing when somebody was about to die. No, she was just psychic, but she understood the laws of karma.

Somehow, she had a feeling this chick here had caught the sights of a succubae.

The door opened not even a heartbeat later.

As the punch of sex, slick power and sweet perfume flooded the air, Vanya reached up and absently touched the silver chain. It held the silver cross that had belonged to Irina.

Okay, big sis...I get a feeling this is it.

The succubae slid Vanya a look, and sure enough, she caught a glimpse of something not quite human peering out from behind those mortal eyes. A typical, well-adjusted human would look at her and want to get the hell away.

Vanya wasn't surprised when several of the girls standing next to Robbi sidled away, putting some distance between themselves and the demon-possessed mortal.

"Score one for me," Vanya whispered.

Of course, Robbi looked at the succubae with a cocked brow, a cocked hip and a cocky smile.

Vanya sighed and glanced at the others.

"You all might want to leave," she said. Then she shifted her gaze to Robbi and smirked. "And you should go home and change—the dress doesn't make you look any sluttier than getting fucked on the hood of some guy's Smart Car, but, sweetie, that color doesn't look good on you anyway."

Robbi went red then white, but Vanya didn't spare her another five seconds.

Looking past her, she stared at the succubae and debated her choices. If she really, really wanted to minimize human contact, she needed the succubae out of here.

And maybe she could let Robbi live another day or two—who knows, the idiot could always grow a brain cell or two.

With an internal sigh, she made a choice and sauntered toward the succubae.

She knew how to appeal to this kind of demon.

After all, she'd been killing them on the sly for years.

But always one-on-one, which required luring them away from the rest.

And there was more than one demon in this club...Vanya could feel them.

With a silent prayer, she made her choice.

She'd been told a few years ago, when the time was right, she wouldn't be alone.

Didn't seem like there would be a better time than now.

Oddly enough, she felt pretty damn alone.

Chapter Two

Then...in years past...

The boy laughed.

Sitting in the sunshine, he'd discovered something amazing.

He could make the sun hide.

It was amazing. It was wonderful. If he wished, the darkness could hide him as well, and when he let the darkness fade, coming back to the sun's bright light was wonderful.

He wanted to show his mother, his father.

They would be so amazed by what he could do.

So amazed...

With a smile, he went to search for them.

It was not long before his smiles and laughter turned to tears and screams.

It took much longer, though, for the screams to be silenced. It took days, or was it weeks...months? Perhaps years?

Once the screams went silent though...they were silent...forever.

Now...

"Where are you going?" Sina asked, watching as Silence packed his things—his weapons. Most of them were axes...he'd always liked his axes.

He answered with a half shrug. Sina knew better than to be bothered by the lack of a better answer. He would know where he was going—Will told him more than he usually told others. Many people did. It was a gift, she supposed, although Silence probably didn't view it as such.

She supposed some people thought it easier to tell their secrets to a man who had no voice. He wouldn't be able to tell those secrets, as least not with his voice. Not that Silence was the kind to share secrets, even if he could speak.

It wasn't just that, though.

Silence had few friends, but there was something about him that compelled others to confide in him, that compelled trust.

Perhaps they looked at him and saw the echoes of the horrors he'd known.

Perhaps they looked at him and knew there was nothing they could say that would shock, horrify or surprise him.

Sina knew that to be true. Nothing horrified him. Nothing shocked him. Nothing surprised him.

Except that was getting ready to change... Silence was in for a surprise, the shock of his life. It wouldn't horrify him, but he wasn't going to welcome this.

Sighing, she rolled onto her belly and stared out the window. As far as the eye could see, there were mountains. Tucked away high in the Rockies, her little cabin was unknown to most people. Silence knew, Will, a few select others. But that was all.

And Silence was the only one she'd welcomed into this bed as a lover.

It hurt her heart to realize that last night had been the end for them.

Part of her wondered if it would make it easier for him if she said something...warned him.

But Silence wouldn't be looking for this.

It was why they had gotten along so well. Neither of them wanted anything more.

Silence needed a woman's warm body, took comfort in Sina's presence when the days stretched on endlessly. But he had no desire for love or anything deeper.

Sina's heart belonged to somebody else.

Yes, they were a good match, neither of them able to promise anything but the pleasure they shared in bed. And friendship.

That friendship was a deep one, strong and true, forged over years...centuries. And she knew him well. Knew the set of his shoulders was tense, knew that his reticence was unusual...even for him.

Sliding from the bed, she walked to him and slipped her arms around his waist.

"You're not happy."

Big, scarred hands covered hers and squeezed gently. He tried to nudge her away, but she wasn't in the mood to be nudged, budged or distracted. Working her way between the bed and him, she caught his face in her hands and made him look at her.

He had the features of an angel—too perfect, far too perfect. His ice-blue eyes met hers as he caught her hands in his.

Gently, he squeezed them then let go, signing to her in a language that only existed for some of the Grimm.

It had been one they had created so they could speak with Silence, this man who was trapped in a silence of his own, his voice gone.

Locked in silence—not a way to spend eternity.

Am I ever happy, my lady?

"This is different," she said, shaking her head.

He sighed, his ice-blue gaze staring off into the distance. His hands moved and Sina watched.

Yes. Something feels—

He paused, shook his head. Then resumed, his big, scarred hands so fluid, so graceful. *Something is different. There is change coming. A darkness looming.*

She wondered at the darkness, although she suspected that was just the change he sensed, and his own misgivings. Once he made it through this, if he could simply accept it, his days wouldn't be taking a turn for the darker, but for the brighter...the better. Lucky bastard.

Her heart ached for her friend as his eyes returned to hers and she saw the fear in his gaze. He'd never admit it, that fear. But she saw it, felt it even as it swelled inside him.

Silence had never handled change all that well...and with the touch of precognition that he had, it was enough for some part of him to realize this change was big. It would make it harder, make him dread it all the more.

Reaching up, she touched his cheek.

"Everything changes. We've lived long enough to know that, lover."

With a soundless laugh, he shook his head. *Yes. Everything changes. And nothing changes. That much I know. But this—*

something feels different. I do not want to go on this mission, Sina. In my soul, I feel that everything is about to change.

"Would that truly be a bad thing?"

He stiffened and pulled away, going to stare out the window. He braced his hands on the sill, bowed his head. With his broad back rigid, he stood there.

She could feel the turmoil inside him, although she didn't allow herself to pry. She didn't need to, truly. As long as she had known him, she suspected she knew what he was thinking.

Slowly, he turned, facing her. His gaze eyes stared into hers, and she saw the torment of centuries of memories burning in his eyes. *Any time my life has taken a drastic change, Sina, has it brought me pleasure? Or more pain?*

Sina didn't answer.

They both knew the answer.

In his mortal life, the first major change in his life had come when he had been a child, and he'd developed those unusual...gifts. Or curses.

He had been brutalized, beaten, tortured by people who thought his unusual abilities marked him as some spawn of Satan. The injuries brought upon him were so grievous they rendered him mute, locked him in silence for eternity.

He would have been put to death, but a so-called man of God had taken him, said he'd try to save the boy's soul. What happened for the next few years were things that Silence had never told anybody.

Sina knew, though, and she knew enough to tell her that unless that so-called man of God had come to see the error of his ways before his untimely death, his sorry ass was burning in hell.

She'd seen the memories locked in the back of Silence's mind, nightmares he never shared. Years of torture, humiliation and horror that ended when he snapped and killed his abuser—another change, one that led to years where he lived alone, hardly more than an animal, unable to speak, hardly seen by people, tormented by his memories, terrified by the gift that had led to all his problems.

Then a chance at happiness, what he'd hoped was friendship, only to be betrayed and imprisoned yet again. A decade, he'd spent locked away, and it was there that Will came to him.

Even the change from mortal to Grimm hadn't been easy—many of the others shied away from the big, strange, silent man...he'd spent too much time on his own in life and rarely interacted with others. Rarely cared enough to try.

And it showed.

No, Silence had every reason to not welcome change.

She understood.

But there was no way she could soothe him. Not now.

If he had any idea what was coming for him, he'd fight it. Perhaps even run from it.

Then...

It was cold.

It was hungry.

The scent of food was the only reason it left the warmth of its cave. The smell of meat cooking tickled something in its mind, something that almost made it smile. It saw somebody in its head, a memory forgotten until that moment. *Mother*...it had called her Mother. It saw her bent over the fire, stirring something that smelled like cooking meat.

Thinking of Mother made its chest hurt.

It hadn't thought of her in so long. Creeping through the forest, it wondered if it could find her.

Dirty hair, so long it almost touched its waist, hung in its face. It did not understand why, but when it passed the water, it stopped and cupped some in its hand, splashed it on its face. *Cold...so cold...*

It didn't matter, though, because Mother liked it clean.

So it did it again and again then twisted, dipped its head in the water. Mother didn't like it when it got dirty. It...

It frowned and peered into the water, waited for the surface to calm. It...

Not *it*.

He.

And *he* had a name...

Mother had called him something...what had she called him?

He did not remember. He closed his eyes, tears burning them. He sniffled, and when he did, the scent of the cooking meat filled his senses again. Made him think of Mother.

Rising, he started to walk.

When he heard the scream, he started to run.

Mother...?

He burst into the clearing, silent as death. His eyes scanned around, searching for Mother. She wasn't there. But he saw a woman, several men—most of the men were dead. The woman was being held down.

Mother...

It wasn't her, but in that moment, it didn't matter.

She had been cooking, and these men wanted to hurt her.

From the corner of his eye, he saw something gleam.

An axe—he knew what it was, for he had seen his father using one many times. Snarling, he grabbed it and lunged.

Now...

When he stepped from Will's pathway, Silence lingered long enough to glance back at his friend.

Will smiled at him. It wasn't much of a smile—hardly one Silence could call reassuring.

"Go on," he said, adding on a name that Silence automatically tuned out. He didn't answer to that name, didn't respond to it—hated to even hear it. He'd been nameless so very long, and then out of the blue Sina had started calling him Silence—Silence was all he would answer to now.

But Will was a bastard who liked to poke at old wounds.

I'm not cut out to teach—how am I to speak to her? he signed, shaking his head.

Will cocked a brow. "You know as well as I do this isn't really something I decide. I do what I'm told—the same as you. But if I was told to send you here, then it was for good reason. Have faith in that."

Silence smirked. Faith. He didn't have faith in much of anything anymore. Faith had fucked him over too many times. But he did trust Will. Mostly. Sighing, he looked toward the warehouse looming over him. He felt the punch of power, evil, lust and death emanating from it—incubae, succubae. Riding high on their power as they sucked it through their drones.

And somewhere in that was his human.

Somebody he was to teach. To train.

After, of course, he'd let him or her die.

This wasn't going to be a fun night.

He broke in through the fourth-floor window.

The punch of their power was stronger here—a lot stronger. It was an arousing, uncomfortable itch that flowed over his skin and stiffened his cock even as it made him wish he had a swimming pool of bleach he could go immerse himself in. That might be enough to clear their noxious power from his pores, but he didn't think so.

At least he no longer had that overpowering effect where he felt like he had to have sex or die—he was immune to that much, at least. Still, he hated succubae, incubae. Damn parasites. Sexual ticks—worse. And there was never just a couple of them because they didn't like to travel in small groups—always had to be in large groups. The weaker ones—the drones—siphoned energy from their lovers and they fed their stolen power to their leader.

It was a living, breathing orgy—an unclean one.

As he made his way through the darkness and silence of the top floor, he drew his axe. Absently, he stroked a thumb along the blade—lightly. Wouldn't do to draw blood. Not this close. They couldn't hear him unless he made noise, and he wouldn't. They couldn't sense him—the Grimm were naturally able to dampen their presence. But drawing blood around a demon—might as well do it in shark-infested waters.

Of course, sharks were a quicker, cleaner way to go.

He extended his senses, focusing. How many…

One. Two—eight. Ten.

He could handle those odds.

And the human—female.

He winced automatically. He'd hoped for a man. He didn't want to train a woman—didn't want to stand by and watch a woman die, either.

A soft voice, low and husky, drifted up. It was a nice voice, he thought. And since it didn't make his eardrums shudder, cringe and long for more Clorox, he already knew whose it belonged to—his human.

"I've got a better idea—why don't you just bite me?"

He snorted and shook his head. Bad words to say to a sex demon—anything that could be taken remotely sexual, they would.

Somebody laughed, and the sound of it made his skin crawl. Worse, the power he felt throb in the air was strong.

The queen—his human was talking to the queen.

Edging to the railing, he peered out of the shadows down to the lower level. It was set up to resemble something like a porn scene. Beds, several of them. A rack that looked part medieval torture device and sex toy—although why a person would willingly go on that, he didn't know. He'd done his time on the real rack and there wasn't anything one could say that would get him back on one, no matter the sexual enticement offered.

His sexual tastes might sometimes run to the perverse, but a rack? No. Just…no. Looking at it, even thinking of seeing his human on it was enough to make him want to use one of his larger axes and hack it into splinters.

His human was being backed up, closer and closer to it.

She had a knife in her hand—long, closer to a sword than a knife, but it wasn't going to do much good against that many of the demonic. The bodies the succubae and incubae possessed became stronger, and even if she could hold her own against a couple…well, ten was too much to ask of any mortal.

Still, there was something about the way she held it that made him think she knew how to use it.

Demons didn't like pain more than anybody else, and they could be killed—not the way mortals could, but if she dealt a killing blow, their souls would be sucked back to the netherplains. It weakened them, and if they survived, it would take them a good long while to try to cross back over into this world.

Sometimes, they *did* die. Silence planned to kill the lot of them tonight.

"Come on, precious," one of them said, giving her a charming, seductive smile. "Put the knife down. You came out here looking for a good time, right?"

She gave him a smile in return. "Well...yes. But my idea of a good time is going to be very different from yours. You see, *my* idea of a good time is to kill as many of you as I can before I die. I'm already up to two." She spun the blade and cocked a brow. "Who's next?"

Despite himself, Silence smiled.

She had guts. More...she knew what was coming. How strange. Odd, that. Perhaps Will had prepared her a bit more than Silence had expected.

One of them lunged for her. She swayed to the side and her knife was a silver flash in the air.

Silence smelled blood in the air. He slid his axe into place and gathered his shadows.

Then he steadied himself. In another few minutes, he'd have to watch her die.

In that moment, he hated Will.

Bracing a hand on the railing, he leaped.

Air rushed along his body, and for a moment, he wished he could hit hard enough, fast enough to end it...end himself so he wouldn't have to see this.

But that was an easy exit that didn't exist for him.

Vanya thought she heard the air whistling—thought she glimpsed something in the darkness. But she didn't dare look. The avid, hungry look in their eyes was already unsettling—now touched with anger. She'd killed two of them earlier.

They didn't just want to fuck her and try to talk her into giving up her soul for the sake of sex now—they wanted her to bleed too.

She had no doubt she was going to bleed, going to hurt.

Shit, where were they? He...she...*somebody*...

She'd been told she wouldn't be alone.

Off in the distance, there was a heavy, deliberate tread.

A footstep.

Something shivered down her spine.

She didn't look—didn't dare.

But some of them didn't have that caution. They looked. And swore.

Something shiny, red and wet flew across her field of vision.

Blood.

There was a shriek of rage and the possessed woman Vanya had first seen in the club bathroom snarled, "What the hell...?"

Another footstep. Deliberately heavy. Deliberately hard. Like whoever moved in the shadows wanted to be heard before he was seen. She squinted, still focusing on the demons, although it wasn't so easy to see them now. Was it her imagination or was it darker in here now?

Vanya tried to catch a glimpse, but then one of the men rushed at her. She slashed with her knife but wasn't quick enough. He had her pinned, trapped against his body, and he was strong—so damned strong. And yes, even now—horny as hell.

One iron hand gripped her wrist, squeezed, squeezed, squeezed... "Drop it, baby," he panted in her ear. "Now, or when I get you naked, after I'm done fucking you with my dick, I fuck you with that."

Pain and terror blossomed in her mind, but still she clutched the blade.

Off in the darkness of the huge room, she caught a glimpse of something—no, somebody. A man—the glitter of his eyes. Nothing about that one glimpse made her shudder with fear. In fact, that one glimpse had something warm and easy rolling through her.

It gave her the courage she needed to gasp through the pain, "I bet the knife does a better job than you."

He shattered her wrist and she screamed with the pain. The blade fell from her useless fingers and he backhanded her, sent her flying to the floor. She landed at the feet of the woman who'd brought her here. She grabbed the front of Vanya's skimpy black dress and yanked her up, but whatever she might have said was cut short by a harsh gasp.

As one, the two women turned their heads, watched as a long, brawny arm came out of the thick, seemingly impenetrable darkness—why was it so dark? A scarred hand grabbed the neck of the demon who had broken Vanya's wrist.

He screamed, but the scream ended abruptly in a wet, nasty gurgle.

His head, sans body, rolled across the floor like a macabre bowling ball, coming to a stop a few feet away from Vanya and the woman.

The woman shrieked and threw Vanya to the floor, staring off into the darkness.

"Who is there?"

Vanya, through the pain, started to laugh.

"You..." The demon looked at her. A furious hiss escaped her and she lunged for Vanya, gripping the bodice of her dress. "Who is there? What have you done, you little cunt?"

Vanya laughed harder. If there was something hysterical to her laughter, it couldn't be helped.

The woman's eyes narrowed and she reached down, touched the silver chain Vanya wore. Something that might have been fear entered her eyes. "You're not..."

Then she grabbed the chain, spilling the silver cross out. And she heaved out a sigh of relief.

"No. You're not what I thought you were."

Abruptly, Vanya stopped laughing. Behind the demon, another two of her men disappeared. Damn, she was losing them left and right, and the bitch was standing here worrying about *Vanya*? Vanya wasn't the damn problem.

Then he was there—bigger than life, his hair the palest blond, his face...damn, that face, it was too beautiful, too perfect to be real, and over one muscled shoulder, he had an axe. Blood dripped from the gleaming silver blade.

Vanya looked at the demon and smiled. "No. I'm not what you thought. But something tells me *he* is."

Her shriek could have made ear drums bleed—Vanya thought hers just might. Then she was too busy worrying about the nausea roiling through her gut as the woman snatched her up, jarring her shattered her wrist. A hand fisted in her hair, jerking her head back so far it was a wonder it stayed attached.

"Get back, Grimm, or the mortal dies."

He didn't say anything, just pointed his axe at another one of the demons—a blond man, one of the few that remained.

The blond gulped, shot the woman a look...and took off running.

Vanya might have laughed.

If she wasn't busy screaming. The demon grabbed her shattered wrist and squeezed, squeezed, squeezed...

Just two left, Silence thought.

The queen was the biggest threat and not just because she held his woman—no. His human. His soon-to-be pupil. The queens, the kings, they were always stronger, and he knew her entire hive hadn't been here. If it had, she'd be wavering now, weaker after he'd killed so many of her slaves.

A king or queen was a strong fighter—able to draw on the strength of the hive and could even call on them through their link, draw them into the fight.

He needed her away from the mortal—preferably *dead*.

Lifting a hand, he beckoned her close.

She smirked. "What am I... stupid? Get back, Grimm, or I break her neck."

She was close to doing that now, Silence thought, straining the woman's neck so far, he knew it must hurt her. That is, assuming, she could think past the pain in her wrist.

Fine. The queen wasn't going to face him—that meant making it clear she had to cut her losses and run, which she wouldn't do until he showed her she had no choice. He skimmed the shadows—seeing through them easily. They were his, after all. He called them and they came. One of his gifts—the gift of illusion, the reason he had been beaten, imprisoned most of his mortal life.

The final drone was out there, cleverly trying to sneak around, holding a gun in his hands. A gun—fool. Tossing his battle axe to his left hand, Silence grabbed one of the two throwing axes he kept on his belt. It whistled through the air, cleaving through the man's skull like a ripe melon.

As he fell down, his body lifeless, Silence released his illusions and let the queen see.

Let her see that she was truly alone...alone with just him.

Not where she wanted to be.

Her eyes went wide—

And then she hissed.

Before she flung the mortal at him, she took a split second to rip her throat out.

Silence closed his eyes for a moment—as far as deaths went, it was a relatively painless way to go.

But fuck it all, he didn't want to see this.

He'd seen enough death to last him through all eternity.

The demon fled as he moved to the woman's side.

He knelt down and took her hand as her life faded.

I'm here, he signed automatically with his free hand, using the language he had first used with Sina and Will all those years ago, the language Will had created just for him. Even as he did it, he wondered why. It wasn't like she could see, as first pain then death glazed her eyes.

Even if she could, she wouldn't understand.

He didn't even know her name.

Not that it would matter to her—it wasn't like he could speak, offer comfort as she went through the change from mortal to Grimm...through death's door and back again.

She would be locked in silence as she made this change, just like he was.

Might as well be alone, for all the good it did having him there.

You're not alone, he thought as he brushed a lock of hair back from her face, still holding her other hand in his. His hands itched to move—itched to echo the words within his mind.

Silence, the silence he'd been trapped in for so long weighed on him, but for some reason, he wanted to hold her hand and keep the other curved where he could stroke the silken skin of her cheek.

Her skin was cooling...her life, already gone.

It was done.

He felt the ripple in the air, that tightening, and he sighed, shaking his head. Why was the bastard coming now?

"Her name is Vanya," a voice said from behind.

Will.

Glancing back at him, Silence lifted a brow.

Sina had once told him he could convey entire conversations with just a look. Perhaps Will agreed because he just shrugged and said, "Well, would you rather stare at her and think of her as *human*—although that won't apply for much longer. Perhaps you intend to think of her simply as *protégée*? Knowing her name will help you both. And I'm here to deal with the mess, because as always, you made a hell of one."

Will nudged one of the heads and scowled. "Off with their heads."

Then he came over and crouched on her other side, across from Silence.

His hand touched her throat—under it, brilliant, bright-white light flared.

Silence looked away.

But from the corner of his eye, he saw Will place a hand on her chest, just over her heart, and he found himself staring down, watching as Will called her back.

Back through death's door.

It wasn't Will's power that made it possible—he was just the channel.

But it was a fucking disconcerting thing to watch.

Chapter Three

Then...

"You cannot kill him!" The woman stood before his body, her arms spread wide.

Mother was not here.

Mother hated him—she thought him evil.

Mother didn't want him. Neither did Father. They had let him be taken—immediately his mind shied away from what had happened, what became of him...what had been done. What *he* had done...

This woman, though, she fought to protect him. To help him. But he doubted she could.

With his arms wrapped around his thin, cold body, he sat on the ground, clutching the axe and staring at the men he'd killed. He still had their blood on him.

The sight of their dead bodies, the sight of the blood brought the memories rushing back.

A fat, foul-smelling man—*I will fight for his soul. I will clean him of this devil curse...*

Pain, so much of it. He shuddered, gripped the axe harder, barely aware of those around him who spoke.

"Your majesty, I strongly suggest you ignore the lady. She is overly emotional. He saw too much."

There was a heavy sigh. "I did not ask for your opinion."

"Sire—"

"He saved our lives. I will not blindly overlook that. Now be *silent.*"

The harsh fury in the man's voice made him cringe as he sat there, shuddering, reliving so many ugly, awful memories. From the corner of his eye, he saw him coming, saw him standing over him.

"Look at me, boy."

He did not dare.

"I said—"

"Oh, stop yelling at him," she said. "Can you not see his fear?"

Then she knelt by him, an angel in pink and gold. Uncaring of the blood on him, she reached out and touched his arm. "Will you look at me, boy? Please?"

He darted a look. Then looked away.

"What is your name?"

He shook his head. A name. He had a name. But he had no way to tell her.

"You have no name?"

He hesitated then shook his head. He had a name. One he did not remember, and even if he did, he could not tell her. Slowly, he reached up and touched his mouth, shook his head, watching her from the corner of his eye, not daring to look directly at her, still hiding behind his damp, dirty hair.

"Oh…you cannot speak." She sighed and looked up. "How can you kill him now? He cannot even tell a soul that he saw you with me, Louis."

The man she called Louis knelt down as well. "Just because he says he cannot speak doesn't mean he cannot speak," the man muttered. "Look at me, boy, and do it now or I will have you killed and be done with it."

He looked—he did not want to die, and somehow he understood this man could have him killed.

So he looked. And something about the face he saw startled him—

The man called Louis sucked in a harsh breath and then looked at his lady.

"Well. Perhaps I could have killed him before I looked at him, but it will be harder now. He shares my face, Françoise. Do you see?"

Abruptly, there was a shout, followed by a scream. The guards came, hustling the lady and the man to the carriage. The woman—Françoise—she reached out and caught his thin arm. "You come too. You have faced enough thieves and bandits this day. Let the guards handle this."

Louis gave her a disapproving frown.

"What? Would you have this boy with your face be slaughtered?"

There was another scream from the guards, and something about it made the skin on the boy's neck crawl.

What came out of the woods were men—or at least they looked like men. But they moved too fast. And they were too strong. The boy had never seen a man who could rip the arms off another man, but that was what one did. The men who guarded Louis and his lady Françoise were being cut down like animals.

One of the bandits...no, this was no bandit. That...that *thing* looked toward them and as he stared into the thing's eyes, his gut turned to water.

Evil...he was staring into the very eyes of evil. There was nothing human in those eyes. *Nothing...*

Without understanding why, he gathered the shadows and used his darkness, spreading it across the clearing.

Françoise screamed.

Knowing he needed to see, the boy eased back and rested a hand on her knee, and one on Louis as well. The darkness eased for them and he saw the shock on their faces. He flinched, prepared himself for what they would say, what they would think, what they would do.

But Françoise gazed at him in wonder.

"Louis, did you see? What he can do?"

"Françoise, be quiet," Louis said, sweat breaking out on his brow. He looked at the boy, his mouth set in a grim line. "If you truly know how to fight, then you should prepare yourself."

He swallowed and looked back. He could not tell the man named Louis that there would be no fighting. He looked over his shoulder at the door to the carriage and then back at Louis.

They needed to escape.

Now.

Louis stared at him, eyes narrowed.

He shot the door another look then gave Louis one more pleading look.

"Very well, boy. I hope you know what you are about..."

Now...

She hurt.

Vanya thought the pain would choke her—either the pain or the blood.

Fear dominated her mind, swamped her.

I'm here, somebody whispered through her mind.

A hand touched her brow.

Strong, gentle.

Then it was gone—

No, she thought desperately. *Please don't leave...*

"I won't leave you alone. I'm here, Vanya."

Who was he? She needed something to cling to during the dark, but she didn't know how to ask, couldn't find her voice to save her life.

And then, as though he'd sensed her need, she heard it again, a vague whisper of thought.

"I am Silence—"

*Silence...*what a strange name.

Her last conscious thought was that he knew her name...and she hadn't been alone, after all.

Silence scowled as he looked around the small, dank hotel room.

It reminded him too much of the squalid little rooms where he had spent much of his mortal life. Too closed in. Not enough windows. Not enough light.

Then he focused his gaze on Will. *This is a hovel,* he signed.

"It's where she's been living for the past few months, my friend. She doesn't have much money and it's the best she's been able to manage."

Cocking a brow, Silence pointed out, *You have money.*

Most of them did.

"And do you really think she's going to let me pay her way? You don't know modern women very well, do you?"

Silence frowned. No. No, he didn't. The woman he knew best was Sina—and *modern*, she was not. She might adopt certain mindsets, certain attitudes and customs, and heaven knew she loved the clothing and conveniences...but modern?

She'd been ancient when *he* had been born.

He dropped his bag on the floor by the wall and eyed the lone, rickety chair at the table. It wouldn't hold his weight. It would shatter into splinters and toothpicks, and then he'd have to pick them out of his own ass.

My home, he signed, looking at Will. *Open your damned doorway—let me take us to my home. She can make her transition there. I can begin her training there.*

"Not yet." Will shook his head. "She'll adjust better if she awakes in familiar surroundings—you know it. Plus..." he blew out a breath, "she needs to say goodbye to her life. Let her have that. A few days, a few weeks, perhaps."

Will grimaced and looked around the hotel room. "Trust me, once she wakes up and her new senses kick in, she's *not* going to want to stay here."

Then he was gone.

Lucky bastard, Silence mouthed, shaking his head. Blond hair fell into his face and he sighed, fishing around in his pocket for a band to pull it back with.

She'd go into the fever soon—the fever always came as the body adjusted to the changes. It would last for hours.

It wasn't an easy process and she was stuck with him. Sighing, he settled at her side and rested a hand on her face, his thumb absently tracing over one of the scars.

Where had they come from? Gently, he angled her face to the side a bit so he could see the marks better. They looked like claw marks almost. Three of them running down the left side of her face.

Vanya moaned, the sound low and tortured.

Looking away from the marks, he saw the look of pain, fear tightening her features.

Not much time.

I'm here, he thought.

It wasn't much, and he knew she couldn't very well hear him.

He went to stroke her midnight black hair from her face, frowning at the blood in it. He needed to clean her up—make her more comfortable.

Now, before the fever started, he supposed.

But as he was washing the blood from her hair, he discovered it wasn't her hair, but a wig.

Scowling, he pulled it away, tossing it aside and combing his fingers through her pale, ash-brown hair. It was shorter, curly, the curls twining around his fingers like silk. It suited her, although he doubted she'd appreciate him thinking so. It made her look as young as he suspected she was. Young...and softer.

The life she faced now was anything but soft.

Then again, he suspected her life hadn't been soft before this.

She had scars, and not just the paltry ones on her face. Scars on her soul, just like him. He imagined the three, thin marks bothered her a lot, although he had seen worse—hell, he *carried* worse, although his own scars weren't as visible as hers.

Lightly, he touched her marks again, one at a time, tracing his finger down each line.

Under his hand, she shivered and he pulled back.

He was supposed to be seeing to her comfort—not pawing her.

The darkness was surreal.

Vanya didn't think she'd ever known a darkness *this* complete.

All encompassing, blacker than any night she'd ever experienced.

But she wasn't afraid.

Not anymore.

Even when the pain came and tore into her with sharp, tearing teeth.

Because she wasn't alone.

He was there.

She didn't know who he was.

She just knew he was there, and that his voice was there to guide her, no matter how dark it got.

"You're safe now, I promise."

"Breathe...just breathe, the pain will pass..."

His words were like a lifeline, circling through her mind, with her no matter how deeply she dreamed, no matter how awful the nightmares became, no matter horrible the pain.

Whoever he was, she felt safer with him than she'd ever felt. Safe, welcome...protected.

Perhaps even *wanted*...

Cared for.

When the fever came, he had a cool cloth to stroke over her brow.

When the dreams were the worst, his voice comforted her, murmuring to her from deep inside her mind, never, never leaving her alone.

When the chills replaced the fever, he warmed her.

When the darkness replaced the nightmares, he stayed by her side, reassuring her.

She wasn't alone.

Not alone—

She flung out a hand and he was there—his hand, bigger than hers, strong and ridged with scars, caught hers, held it.

"I'm here." The voice In her mind was deep, dark and quiet, strong as iron and soft as velvet. *"I'm here and I will not leave you."*

Vanya sighed. And slept.

Then...

"Very good!" Françoise clapped her hands and leaned over, watched as he painstakingly spelled out his name—or rather, the name they had chosen to give him. "You learn so fast. You are terribly clever."

He smiled at her then looked away as blood rushed up his neck, staining his cheeks red.

The past few days with this lady had been the happiest he had known since he had been a small boy.

Before he had made the horrid mistake of telling his mother what he could do. He had thought she'd be amazed and she'd been horrified. He'd feared letting Françoise and Louis know, but they hadn't feared him. He couldn't make sense of it.

There was a sound at the door and he looked up, automatically flinching at the sight of another person. It was Louis. A man he wanted to think was his friend. A man he wanted to be his friend. Nervous, he smiled.

Louis smiled back.

It was a smile that made him feel warmer inside. It was a smile he liked, one he wanted to trust.

And because he wanted to so badly, he did.

It was a mistake that would cost him his freedom for the next ten years.

He could still hear her arguing.

"You cannot do this to him, Louis. It is not right—he *trusted* you!"

"He trusts me *to a point*," Louis snapped.

"Have you forgotten he saved our lives?"

He huddled against the stone wall, staring out the narrow slit of a window, at the nighttime sky, wishing he was back in the forest. Away from here. Away from them, even Françoise. If he was back there, he wouldn't be a prisoner.

Again...

"Have you forgotten we are at war? That we constantly face those who would seek to destroy us? That *boy* is a formidable weapon and he *will* aid me when I need it."

No, he thought, shaking his head. *I will not.*

"You would use him. After he saved us. After he saved *me.*"

There was a pause, and then Louis said, "Françoise, I will do what I must. Please, understand..."

"No. I love you, but I cannot understand this."

There was silence, and then the door opened.

He did not turn his head to look. It was Louis. The man he wanted to call friend.

But he had no friends.

He could trust nobody.

"I did not wish to do it this way," Louis said quietly. "Just tell me you will offer me aid and we will find another way."

He stayed quiet, gazing out at the stars.

There was a sigh at the door. "You will change your mind. In time."

But he did not. Years passed, and he remained locked away...alone. In time, he realized it was best that way. Safer.

Now...

She slept now, Silence thought, studying her face.

A healing sleep, finally.

Her hand still clutched his. There had been times when her short, neat nails had bit into his flesh, times when she had squeezed so tightly, he'd felt the bones of his hand grinding together. She hadn't hit full-strength yet—a good thing because, otherwise, she might have shattered every bone in his hand.

Not that he would have stopped her. It wouldn't have been the worst pain he'd ever dealt with, and if it brought her some comfort...

Sighing, he reached for the rag and once more stroked it over her damp brow. A few more hours, he thought, and she'd awaken.

Then things would really get interesting for her.

How much did she know?

Sometimes, Will had explained things well.

Other times, not so much.

He hoped she had at least more than a vague idea of what was going on. She certainly had been aware of her impending death, although that simply could have been premonition. She'd known about them, though. Will never brought one over without offering a choice.

All of them knew *basically* what would come. But sometimes the basics were all they were given—a choice would be made. Do you live and help others? Do you die and move on?

Let it be more than that, he thought.

Absently, he reached up to touch his medallion through his shirt, thought of calling Will.

But he didn't.

Will had already done everything he was going to do.

If there was more he was going to do, he would have already done it.

It was up to Silence now.

Frankly, this woman ought to be scared to death... Having things placed in his scarred hands. *Damn you, Will.*

He didn't want her scared, didn't want her to come into this unknowing...

He'd have to explain—have to think of the best way to make certain she knew all she needed to know.

At first, Vanya thought she might still be dreaming.

Not a nightmare this time, though.

Or maybe she *had* died...died and gone to heaven. Or some sort of way station. It made sense.

Because there was somebody not too far away who looked too perfect to be real.

He stood by the window, staring outside, giving her a look at his profile, and what a pretty, pretty profile...carved cheekbones, nice nose, a rather biteable-looking mouth. His hair was pulled back, leaving her view of that face unobstructed.

She could have happily looked at him for another ten, twenty minutes.

Hell, another ten, twenty hours. Weeks...months. Even years.

But he noticed her attention, and his eyes, the pale, pale blue of a Siberian Husky's, cut her way.

Vanya tensed, bracing herself for the typical reaction she got from most men. The way they'd looked her over in that appraising sort of way, right up until they saw her scars.

But he only stared into her eyes.

Slowly, her heart pounding in her chest, she sat up.

Her mouth was dry, too dry. Spying an unopened bottle of water on the bedside table, she grabbed it and opened it. Her hand shook uncontrollably as she lifted it, though, splattering it all over her clothes. Blood rushed to her face.

A shadow fell across her and she looked up, her breath freezing in her lungs as she realized he was there.

He...who was he?

Silence—

His hand closed over hers, steadying it and guiding it to her lips.

Gratitude flooded her, even as the blush deepened.

So weak, she couldn't even manage to a drink on her own.

The water rushed down her parched throat and she drained the bottle in seconds.

"Ahhh...thank you."

He nodded and backed away, taking the bottle with him and tossing it away.

Studying him, acutely aware of the damp shirt clinging to her, she shifted on the bed. "So...are you...um..."

He gave her his back for a moment, and she fell silent, staring at him as he crouched down, rummaging around for something. When he stood, she saw that he held a laptop and little velvet pouch.

The pouch he held out to her.

The laptop he held in one big hand.

Still feeling as weak as a kitten, Vanya reached for the pouch and watched as he sat on the bed across from hers. Waiting, it seemed.

She opened the pouch and poured what it held into her hand.

Silver.

It heated in her hand, pulsed...throbbed, like it held a life of its own.

She caught the disc it held in her hand, rubbed her thumb over it. Her breath hitched in her chest as the wings etched into the silver glowed.

"Whoa," she whispered.

So finely done...she could see individual feathers carved into the silver. Around the edge of the disc, she saw letters...words her brain couldn't quite process.

Her heart skipped a beat as she looked up at him.

"Well, that answers the question I was going to ask," she said, giving him a weak smile. "I was wondering if you were supposed to be my guide or trainer or whatever."

He gave a single nod.

"You're not much for talking, are you?"

His mouth twitched. Then he opened the laptop.

In the back of her mind, she thought she heard a whisper, a voice...familiar...

"...not right...so sorry, Vanya."

Scowling, she stuck a finger in her ear and wiggled it, watching as he started to tap on the keys. Then he held turned the laptop around so the screen faced her.

I cannot speak. We'll be together for a while. If you wish, I'll teach you to sign so I can speak to you.

Sign...

Vanya blinked. Then, shaking her head at the irony, she lifted her hands and signed to him, slowly, haltingly. *I understand some. My grandmother was deaf and we used it with her. But it's been years since I used it.*

His brows, a few shades darker than his silvery-blond hair, arched over those lovely, pale blue eyes. *Well, that will help.*

But then he started signing—far too fast for her to keep up with.

"Slow down," she begged, shaking her head. "I told you, it's been years since I've had to use any sign."

He did, starting over.

But she still had a hard time concentrating because, once more she heard a whisper in the back of her mind.

"At least...some sense...nice..."

Trying to block it out, she stared at his hands, trying to follow him, even as her brain was trying to follow something else.

You'll feel weak for a while still. You'll have to eat a lot, rest a lot.

Forcing a smile, she said, "It won't be hard to rest. I feel like I could sleep for a week."

You may well sleep most of the next week. You need to eat then you should go back to sleep.

She nodded. "That sounds like a plan. But...um...what do I call you? What's your name?"

In the back of her mind, even before she saw his reply, she heard a voice murmur, "*Silence. I am Silence.*"

She shivered.

Chapter Four

Then...

He had been alone for so long.

He'd forgotten how long.

At first, Louis had come—in secret, of course. *I am not doing this to be cruel, boy. But you have no place to go...I merely want to make sure you are safe.*

So you lock me away? he'd written to him once.

Louis had looked away, but not before the boy saw his guilt. *This is not how I would have wished it. But I asked for your help. You would not give it. Are you ready to help me now?*

No. He would not give the sort of help Louis wanted.

So, he remained locked away, a hidden secret revealed only to Louis. Well, Françoise knew, but she never once returned to visit. And he did not fault her for that—*he* would not return there either, were he in her place.

Save for Louis, no other ever saw him. He saw no other.

So, it was something of a shock for him to wake one night and see a man in his room.

A man who was *not* Louis.

A man with silver eyes, a man who wore all white, a man who spoke of promises, angels, death and second chances.

A man who disappeared…in the blink of an eye.

Now…

Dying was hard enough.

Coming back to life was brutal.

But none of that compared to the hell that Silence had in store for her.

She didn't know where they were—it was a big, empty, open warehouse, somewhere in the middle of downtown Ann Arbor, and every night for the past four nights, they'd been coming here.

Coming here so Silence could calmly, collectedly pummel her into a broken, whimpering puddle of useless flesh.

It was pathetic.

She'd spent the past seven years of her life kicking ass, taking names…or so she thought.

In the past four days, he'd shown her that she didn't know *shit* about kicking ass.

She was utterly humiliated.

Well, no.

Actually, she was utterly amazed.

Because just watching him, even if it was from the view of flying through the air to land flat on her back, was sheer amazement.

She hadn't known people could *move* like that.

Hadn't known it was possible.

Especially not somebody as big as he was. He should make noise, should move slow. No. Not Silence.

She was also acutely aware of the fact that she was developing something that might have been called a crush on him...except it was a hell of a lot more than that.

A huge hand thwacked her on the side of the head, and she swore, jerked away, glaring at him.

"What the hell...?"

He signed, *You're not paying attention.*

Vanya narrowed her eyes.

"I damn well am paying attention," she snapped. She was just paying attention to the wrong damn thing—like the fact that she really appreciated how he looked in those loose black pants he wore while he kicked her ass. Just the black pants too—he'd shucked the shirt awhile ago, and sweat gleamed on his pale, scarred flesh.

The scars—where in the world had they all come from? He had them *everywhere* too, except his neck up. Some were longer than others, some were more hideous than others. And all of them were old. Just looking at them made her ache in sympathy for the pain he must have suffered. It made her furious, made her want to hurt somebody...or somebodies...as in everybody who had ever left a mark on him.

She wanted to do nothing more than stare at him, but she suspected he'd clobber her if he knew her attention was wandering, so she backed away, forced her attention to focus.

They were talking weapons today.

Weapons, for crying out loud.

The most she ever did with weapons was to carry a big knife.

In front of her, spread out over the floor, there was a slew of weapons—mostly axes—Silence really seemed to like axes.

But there were also some swords, nunchukas, several different styles of knives and staffs.

She touched the staff at the end, stroking her finger down it.

"Walk softly and carry a big stick," she murmured.

Silence reached down, closed a hand around it.

He snapped his fingers and she glanced over. It wasn't necessary for him to do a damn thing to get her attention, but she wasn't about to tell him that—wasn't about to tell him that she was making it a hobby to quietly watch him without him noticing.

He held the staff in front of him, twisted it.

Immediately the staff expanded, from roughly four feet to six, and now there were blades on either end.

"Oh, now that's cool," she said, grinning.

He twirled it, making the silver blades gleam in the air. Abruptly, he stopped and then twisted it again, causing the staff to retract on itself. The blades were gone just that easily. He signed to her. *Like it?*

"It's damn cool. That doesn't mean I can use it."

Not now, no. The point is learning to use it—you need to find some weapons that appeal. Killing demons with your bare hands isn't how you want to do it. Pick a weapon—master it.

She eyed the staff then looked at the rest of the weapons.

The swords, maybe. The axes were out of the question. She didn't feel comfortable even thinking about them. Knives, sure. But the staff...she did like the staff. "If I had to pick one I'm interested in, I'd say the staff," she said, nodding toward it.

He laid it back down. *I'll get you one made, then. It will have to be designed for your height—that one was made for me. For now, we'll practice with the knives.* He smiled at her before bending down and grabbing a couple of knives. *I saw that you already know your way around them.*

She grimaced.

Something told her he wasn't just going to have her going through a few motions.

Silence took this training thing seriously...and since she healed stupid quick now...

"This is going to involve me bleeding at some point, isn't it?" she asked glumly.

Do you plan on letting me get that close?

"Plan on it? No. But somehow I don't think I can stop you." She sighed and took the blades he offered. Then, before he could make the first move, she lunged.

At least she'd get a point in, she thought.

His grin flashed at her as he blocked it.

"Damn," she muttered. "Almost."

She'd almost had him, Silence thought, as he backed away.

She was a natural with a knife.

He wasn't surprised she'd gone for the bladed staff, either.

Just as he wasn't surprised she hadn't liked any of his axes. They didn't appeal to a lot of the Grimm. He liked the axe because it had been his first weapon, but not everybody could use one well.

Vanya eyed him warily as she eased around, moving away from the table—and the rest of the weapons.

Smart girl, he thought. Earlier, he'd let her disarm him and she'd had a brief moment of victory, but they'd been close enough to the table that he'd immediately rearmed himself—with a sword.

She'd only held a knife.

Then, they hadn't drawn blood.

He wasn't going to go so easy on her this time.

Going easy on a student was a sure way to see them in an early grave. She could still die. He wouldn't let it happen.

He'd watched it once.

As much as it bothered him on a very deep level, he ignored it and set about doing what he'd been brought here to do—teach her.

Her eyes went wide the first time he cut her.

She got pissed the second time.

By the third time, when blood was making it hard for her to grip the knife, he was about ready to call it off—he'd done enough, and he had to admit, he was impressed. She was quick.

Very quick.

Silver flashed—big brown eyes glinted.

And he hissed out a breath as Vanya was suddenly pressed against him, her knife lodged against his belly, the tip barely penetrating.

"I think this means I got the next point," she said, smirking at him.

There was blood on her face, just a smudge, from where she'd wiped the sweat from her eyes.

He lifted a hand, without even realizing it, thinking to wipe that blood from her face. Thinking about...

No. He couldn't think about that.

Closing his hand into a fist, he nodded.

Taking a step back, he gestured to the weapons.

She cocked a brow.

"Damn, you're letting me off easily," she said.

Yes.

Because he needed some distance.

Before he did something foolish...he'd almost kissed her.

Silence hadn't played slice and dice today, but damn it, she almost wished he had—if he'd pushed a little harder, she might have worked herself into unconsciousness.

She *hurt*.

Hell, if she were still human, she doubted she would have lived through what he'd done to her.

A month.

They'd been at this for a month and she still didn't feel like she was making any progress.

Damn it.

He was worse than any drill sergeant on earth—she was certain of it.

She swore in a language she barely even understood as she stumbled into the little hotel room, the hulking shadow close at her heels.

She shivered as she thought she heard a quiet laugh in the back of her mind. Each day, it seemed, she heard him clearer. She wondered if she really *did* hear him...or if she was going nuts.

Although part of her dreaded looking, she couldn't stop herself, and when she peered at him over her shoulder, his eyes were bright with amusement and there was a wicked smile on his face.

"What are you laughing at?" she snapped. She tried to pretend she wasn't all but staggering over to the bed, but she doubted she'd fooled him. He knew damn well he'd worked her over. She felt like something that had been dead—*completely* dead—for a week.

As she sat on the edge of the narrow double, she looked at him, but he shook his head. The amusement in his eyes hadn't faded a bit.

"What?"

He lifted his hands, started to sign, and then abruptly stopped—shaking his head.

And if she wasn't mistaken, there was a faint blush creeping up his cheeks.

"*What*, damn it?"

He rolled his eyes and then signed to her.

You just called me a fucking whore.

Vanya clamped a hand over her mouth, tried not to laugh. Okay—she knew her grasp of Russian was admittedly pretty damn shoddy. Ever since her father had died, there wasn't really anybody to speak it with. He'd died when she was young. Too young. Both she and her sister had been raised to speak both languages, and in school, naturally, they'd spoken English. They'd preferred to use English with each other, for the most part. With Grandma, they'd used an odd mix of ASL, Russian and English, and a mix of Russian and English with their father.

And he hadn't *ever* taught them *those* words—they were just words she'd remembered hearing from him occasionally— usually in a fit of anger, along with other colorful phrases.

"Well, that's sad," she drawled, finally lowering her hand. "You speak it better than I do." Then she winced, blood rushing to her cheeks. "Oh, shit, I didn't mean it like that I'm so sorry."

He smiled. *Why? I don't speak. It would be pointless to get upset over a casual remark and pointless for you to have to walk on eggshells and watch every single word you say.* He dumped the large leather duffel he'd been carrying onto the floor and sat on the bed across from her, eying her closely. *You're tired.*

"I'm fine."

You're tired. Too tired. I've told you, it will take you a few months to completely adjust, and I'm pushing you hard with your training. You are allowed to be tired. He pointed to the phone and the neat stack of take-out menus he'd collected from somewhere. *Pick out somewhere to order food from.*

Vanya's belly chose that exact moment to growl, even though the last thing she needed to be doing was ordering takeout. Her money was running pretty damn slim, and somehow it didn't seem right that she keep stealing the way she'd always done. Granted, she'd taken money from those who wouldn't need it—namely the demons she'd killed—but still. She was supposed to be an angel now—a guardian angel. Angels shouldn't steal. "Ah, maybe I could run to the store and pick up some stuff for us to keep around here…"

Silence lifted a brow. *Like you did last week?* He opened his mouth and mimed gagging himself. *If I never see Ramen noodles again, it will be too soon. No, you need to eat—real food, Vanya.*

"Look, I don't have much money…"

Silence lifted a brow. *I'll pay for it. After all, it's only fair. I'm sharing the room. I'll handle the meals.*

She should argue more…

But she was pretty damn tired of Ramen noodles, peanut butter and all that crap herself.

Still, feigning reluctance, she reached for the menus.

Well, one nice thing—there wasn't a shortage of decent places to eat in Ann Arbor. Nice thing about college towns. It meant there were plenty of places that offered takeout. She settled on Italian, figured her body could use the carbs. Silence had told her she'd be very hungry for the first few months, her body replenishing the reserves she'd depleted while she went through the change.

While she was studying the menu, she was vaguely aware of Silence rising from the bed, vaguely aware of him moving around the room—although he didn't make a sound.

He was so damn quiet—*Silence* was an appropriate name for him, all right.

Wavering between the fettuccini alfredo and the lasagna, fighting the heavy weight of her tired body, she sighed. That voice—the one that had her convinced she was going out of her mind—was there in the back of her head again, murmuring, muttering...

"I push her too hard. She looks too tired. I should let her rest more."

"I'm fine," she said absently.

Then she stiffened and lifted her head, all too aware of his sudden, intent interest. Swallowing, she met his pale blue gaze.

His eyes narrowed.

Blood rushed to her cheeks.

"Um...nothing." She looked back at the menu in her hands, tried to ignore the voice.

It was harder, though—because now his voice was *louder*.

More focused.

And now, he was calling her by name.

"Do you hear me, Vanya?"

Pointedly, she ignored it. Lasagna, she thought. She really thought she could use some lasagna. It had been a while since she'd had a good dish of lasagna. And after all, he was buying, right? Bread too. Salad. Yeah. That sounded good.

"Vanya, look at me."

She started to whistle as she reached over and grabbed a pen and a notepad from the bedside table.

"You'll have to figure out what you want and then I'll call it in," she said, forcing more cheer than she actually felt into her voice.

"Just order me what you're getting."

"Okay, two—"

Fuck.

Her hand tightened on the pen, and then she carefully laid it down before she looked over at him.

He was eyeing her closely, a narrow, appraising look on his face.

"You hear me," he said pointedly.

"Ah...well, not all the time," she hedged. Licking her lips, she looked at the menus and then laid them back down, sighing. "I just...hell, I thought I was going crazy or suffering some weird, post-death, come-back-to-life thing."

That deep, rumbling laughter whispered through her mind, and a wide grin split his face.

"Exactly how often do you hear me?"

"Shit," she muttered, shifting around on the bed. Sighing, she tucked her hair back behind an ear. From the corner of her eye, she saw the menus. Seizing on that distraction, she shoved one toward him. "Aren't we going to eat? I'm hungry."

He lifted a brow.

It was amazing how many things he could say with simply a look.

Still, she didn't look away, didn't lower the menu.

He signed, *I already said, whatever you're having. Order. Then we talk.*

Naturally, it only took two minutes to place the order—nowhere near enough time for her to get her thoughts straight.

The past month had been hard, grueling—she didn't even know it was possible for a person to be beaten into the dirt as often as he had. It didn't necessarily help that come morning, her body felt completely refreshed, completely revitalized…meaning he came at her just as hard, just as fast.

She'd rather they start a fresh bout of training all over again than to have any sort of…*talk.*

Especially something remotely personal.

After she laid the phone back in the cradle, she looked back at Silence.

The two of them, they hadn't done much talking, at least not of a personal nature. Lots of training. He'd done a lot of explaining about what sort of demons they'd face—succubae, incubae, orin…others. How they traveled from a place called the netherplains to their world—most of them had to take over a human body in order to do much of anything.

Basically, she played student to his teacher—if there was a theme song for her new life, maybe it could be "Hot for Teacher".

He made her heart race just looking at him.

He also made her belly clench, made her palms go damp, her knees go weak.

He made her ache.

In the worst possible way, in the sweetest way.

And now he wanted to talk about her gifts.

Hell. This was too damn personal.

What if he was like her?

She'd gotten pretty damn good at hiding how she felt over the past few years, but if he was anything like her...

Vanya blushed even thinking about it. Blushed furiously as she sat there with her chest tight, her palms sweaty, her breath lodged in her throat.

"You've got gifts, don't you?" she blurted out.

Silence narrowed his eyes. *We're supposed to be talking about your gifts,* he signed. He added emphasis by jabbing a finger at her after he'd finished. *Yours.*

"I know. I just...well, this is weird. I haven't talked to anybody about what I can do. It's..."

The hard line of his mouth softened and the aggravated look in his blue eyes faded. *Not easy to talk about, is it?* he signed.

"No." She hitched a shoulder up, wondered how she could explain that she barely even needed him to sign when he was talking to her because she often heard his voice—low and deep—in the back of her mind. And if he was *thinking* about her, she heard him too.

How did she tell him that?

He sat down next to her. She had to check the impulse to scoot away—the long, hard length of his thigh against hers made her uneasy—made her want to climb into his lap, see if she couldn't crack the polite, friendly mask he wore around her.

He held out a hand. Startled, she looked at it—stared at his broad, scarred palm. His hands were a mess—ridged with scars that looked like knife cuts, burns, other old injuries she couldn't even indentify. So at odds with his perfect, angelic face. Looking from that scarred hand into ice-blue eyes, she said, "What?"

He grinned. And again she *heard* his thoughts. *"You want to know about my gifts. I'll show you."*

Nervously, she laid her hand in his. "You're not a psychic, are you?"

He shook his head, and then with his free hand, gestured to the room.

Vanya looked around. "I don't know what I'm looking for..."

He took his hand away.

The room fell into darkness. Darkness so complete, she couldn't even see him, although he sat right next to her. She couldn't *feel* him, and she'd gotten pretty damn good at that.

Then his hand was in hers again, and the darkness was gone.

"Oh—"

Once more he pulled his hand away.

The darkness returned.

"—shit."

This time, the darkness didn't disappear. It gradually bled away, like the night bled into day. Her heart banged hard against her ribs as she looked at him.

"What in the hell was that?"

He smiled and signed. She didn't recognize it, though.

When he spoke into her mind, she stiffened. *"It's illusion. I can make you think you see darkness when there is none."*

She blinked. "You mean, it wasn't really dark?" Scowling, she remembered the night at the warehouse—the night she died. "That night. At the warehouse."

Absently, she reached up and touched her throat. She couldn't remember much of anything beyond that first pain, the shock of it. But she remembered everything right *up* to that point...the fear, the terror. The helplessness—knowing she'd been alone.

But she hadn't been.

He'd been there.

Waiting.

Part of her wanted to rebel at the thought—wanted to demand to know why he hadn't done something—even though she already knew the answer. He'd done exactly what he'd been sent to do.

She couldn't very well become one of them if she hadn't died, could she?

And just as she'd been promised, she hadn't been alone.

"That night at the warehouse," she said again. "There was so much darkness. But it wasn't darkness, was it? It was you."

He nodded. A grim look entered his eyes. *"You know that I couldn't have stopped what happened—not if you're meant to be one of us. But I cannot blame you if you are angry."*

"I know that." She sighed and looked away. Bracing her elbows on her knees, she covered her face and said it again. "I know that. It doesn't mean it's easy to *think* about, although...well, it helps knowing I wasn't alone."

She shot him a faint smile. "I was terrified, thinking I was alone."

"You weren't." He touched the back of her hand. His mouth twisted as he studied her face. *"It wasn't easy to simply stand there, either. Even knowing what was to come."*

She blew out a breath. "Well, it's over and done, right?" Self-preservation had her forcing some distance between them.

Sitting there, so close, was wreaking havoc on her state of mind, not to mention what it was doing to her body. "So, the darkness in there that night—that was all you?"

Silence nodded and made that unusual sign, the one she didn't recognize. As he did it, he said in her mind, *"Illusion. Just illusion. It's one of my gifts."*

"That's pretty cool," she murmured, smiling.

He shrugged. Then he reached up, tapped her brow, waiting with a lifted brow.

She grimaced. Standing, she moved away from him, slicking her damp palms down the front of her pants. They were snug-fitting black yoga pants—something Silence had picked up for her. Along with several other changes of clothes—more yoga pants, close-fitting sport bras, the sort of clothes she could maneuver in while he pounded her into the floor.

"I'm psychic," she said, keeping her back to him, staring out the window into the night. "It's not exactly reliable, and usually I've never gotten anything more than the odd random thought here and there. It was strongest with my sister. After she died, it got more erratic—more like a radio station I couldn't quite get to tune in. It was awful when I was in crowds—like I was hearing all these screaming voices and I couldn't focus on any of them."

The muscles at the base of her neck were tight. Reaching up, she cupped a hand over it, rolled her head first one way then the other, trying to ease the tension there, but it didn't help.

She was still a mess of nerves.

A mess of need.

She didn't hear him—

She felt him.

He was there, that big, powerful body heating hers through and through. His hand came up, lightly brushed hers. As if asking permission.

Get the hell away from him before you do something really, really stupid, Van, she told herself. *Like throw yourself at him.*

But when he gently nudged her hand out of the way, she couldn't find the strength to do anything but stand there.

"And the gift is different now, isn't it? Is more powerful? Other changes since you came back?"

She shivered at the low, velvety rumble of his voice echoing through her mind. Or maybe it was the way his roughened skin rasped over her neck as he dug his thumbs into her skin and started to massage away the tension there. Heat blossomed inside and she swallowed the moan before it could escape.

"Yeah," she said, surprised at how steady, how calm her voice sounded. "It's changed, although I don't know if I can say it's more powerful exactly. Most of the change seems to be related to you—I can hear your voice, and you sound clearer than anybody else ever did. The few times we've been around other people...well, there's not much change there. Although that could be because I'm not around them much. There are times when I hear your voice as clearly as if you're talking to me, and the more time that passes, the clearer it gets."

His hands never stilled, and although she couldn't pick apart the individual thoughts, they were in the back of her head, like the dull hum of a conversation she could barely hear.

Finally, he asked, *"When does it seem to be the most clear?"*

"When you're thinking about me. Or like now—if you're talking *to* me." His thumb hit a particularly tight spot to the right of her neck, and despite herself, she groaned. Then, as he focused on that knot of tension, she let her head fall forward, all but sagging against the cool, glass window.

"But not all the time?"

"No. And I think if you try to *keep* me from hearing you, I wouldn't hear you," she said, frowning as she focused and tried to pick up the trail of his thoughts and discovered she couldn't.

She could still hear that dull roar of his thoughts, but nothing she could pick apart and focus on.

"*This is interesting. We should see who else it works on,*" he said.

Absently, she murmured, "I told you, I don't hear others this clearly." But she was too focused on what else she was picking up from him...something warm, bright...an oddly shimmering thing. Emotion, she realized. One she could only describe as pleasure. Happiness, even.

Without understanding why, she somehow knew he was...happy. Pleased. Slipping away from his hands, she turned around and stared up at him, studying him. "You're happy about this," she said, frowning.

Something akin to surprise flashed through his eyes. Then he shut it down and that odd warmth she'd been feeling was abruptly cut off. He lifted a brow and signed, *What makes you think that*?

"The fact that I was feeling it from you?" she said, shrugging. "It doesn't make much sense to me—if somebody told me they were hearing *my* thoughts, I think I'd be pissed."

She went to edge around him, but he caught her arm.

"*You haven't been locked in silence for hundreds of years, Vanya. I have. Having somebody who can hear me at all, well, it's not unpleasant. It isn't as though I cannot block you out, as you've already pointed out. I imagine it's somewhat discomfiting for you, however.*"

His pale blue eyes held hers. There was something so raw in that look—so intimate, so unsettling.

Without realizing what she planned to do, she reached up and touched a hand to his throat, felt the warmth of his skin, the slow, steady beat of his pulse under her thumb.

"It's not discomfiting," she said quietly, stroking her thumb over his skin.

"This doesn't bother you?"

His eyes...damn it, she was getting lost in his eyes...

Vanya's dark gaze locked with his.

He could hear her heart racing.

Could hear the slight hitch in her breathing.

And when she reached up and touched his skin, her palm against his neck, he watched the brown of her eyes darken to black.

"No," she said quietly, her voice husky. "It doesn't bother me."

Careful to keep up a mental shield, he thought, *Let her go now. Put some distance between you...*

This was his student. Just a month past her death. Just a child.

No, she wasn't a child.

Despite her youth—she was twenty-three, young even by mortal standards—there was a wisdom in her eyes. But still, he couldn't be doing this.

She went to withdraw her hand, but suddenly, Silence couldn't stand for her *not* to be touching him. He needed her hands on him, needed her to touch him.

Need…one he'd ignored for far too long.

He caught her hand, pressed it back to his neck.

Then he caught the back of her head.

Watching her eyes, watching for any sign that this was unwelcome, unwanted, he slowly lowered his head.

Vanya's eyes went wide.

Her tongue slid out, trailing across her lower lip, and Silence dipped his head, followed that path with his own tongue. Her nails curled into his neck, bit into his skin, and he shuddered. Wrapping an arm around her, he stroked a hand down her back, palmed her ass and brought her hips against his.

She groaned into his mouth, and he swallowed the sound down, used his tongue to tease her lips apart, desperate to see what other sounds he could coax from her. Would she whimper, would she sigh, would she scream…?

Desperate to find out, he lifted his head and stared at her.

Holding her gaze, he reached for the zipper that held the snug-fitting jacket she wore closed over her lithe torso. As he tugged it down, he lowered the shields on his mind and focused his thoughts, *"Do I stop?"*

A faint flush turned her cheeks pink.

"Stop?" she whispered.

"Yes…stop. I shouldn't do this—I know I shouldn't. But I'm having a hard time convincing myself of that. Do you *want me to stop?"*

Vanya whispered, "No." Her teeth caught her lower lip as she lowered her head, staring at his hand as he dragged the zipper all the way down.

When he went to push the short black jacket back off her shoulders, she looked back up at him, her hands coming up, curling in the material of his white T-shirt.

Silence held still as she pushed it up as high as she could then he stripped it the rest of the way off.

The silver medallion he wore caught briefly in the shirt before falling to rest on his chest. Vanya leaned against him, her hands stroking down over his sides, up over his chest. Her fingers tangled in the light dusting of hair over his chest, tugged.

Silence gritted his teeth against the sweet pleasure and then caught her wrists, eased them down.

His blood burned hot—need was a scream in his head. Had to slow down—had to. Catching the thick band at the bottom of her sports bra, he slowly peeled the sturdy material away. Then he went to his knees, pressed his lips to the faint red marks it had left behind on her narrow rib cage.

A sigh escaped her. She curled an arm around his head, bent hers low over him.

This was happening—really happening.

Too fast—way too fast.

Yet still not fast enough, she thought as he slowly peeled her out of her pants. Each move so slow, so deliberate, as though he was either giving her plenty of time to change her mind...or plenty of time to think about what was coming.

Change her mind—*not* possible, because that would require thought and she couldn't think when he was around.

He was still wearing the sturdy black fatigues that seemed to be his standard uniform, kneeling in front of her as he eased her feet out of the puddle of stretchy black cloth.

Kneeling...that blond hair spilling over his broad shoulders, his head bent, his hands now resting on her ankles.

When he started to stroke up, her breath caught in her throat.

As his fingers brushed over the backs of her calves, she shivered.

When he reached her knees, he nudged her legs wider. Bracing her hands on his shoulders, she let him guide her feet to where he wanted. But as he leaned in, pressed his face to her, she still wasn't prepared.

Not for the rough-velvet rasp of his tongue over her flesh, and not for the blistering heat of hunger that shuddered out of him, breaking over her—too much—

"*Vanya...*"

She sobbed, and if he hadn't been holding her, she would have fallen. Only the solid, unrelenting grip of his hands at her hips, the cool glass of the window at her back kept her upright.

His nose brushed against her clit just before his tongue speared through her folds, licking, stroking.

"Silence..." she whimpered, fisting a hand in his hair.

He shifted slightly, curled his tongue around her clit and started to suck on it. She felt each rhythmic pull in her very center, felt the heat building.

Silence stroked a hand up her thigh—she felt the ridges of his scars, felt the rasping over her flesh, another sensation over too many sensations. Lightly, he teased her entrance with a fingertip, teased her, stroked her...and when he slowly pushed two fingers inside, she slammed her head back against the window and came with a sob.

His voice was a muted rumble in her mind, one she could barely understand as she shuddered through the climax, shuddered, shook and tried to breathe. Just when she thought she'd be able to manage one decent breath of air, Silence stood, wrapped one arm around her waist, pulling her against him.

Belatedly, she realized they'd been pressed against the window—where anybody could see. She couldn't quite work up the interest to care, though, not when his mouth was teasing hers again, not when he was kissing her, his teeth nibbling at her lower lip tauntingly, then his tongue was sliding over hers, stroking and twining and teasing...

With awkward, shaking hands, she reached between them and fumbled for his zipper. She finally managed to get her fingers to cooperate and she dragged it down, shaking as her fingers brushed against him—thick, hard, throbbing under the restraint of his pants.

When she shoved a hand inside and closed her fingers around him, she felt and heard his reaction—blistering-hot want exploded through a mental connection, followed closely by, *"Stop or this will end before we even start."*

Tearing her mouth away from his, she whispered against his lips, "Then we just start all over again..."

He caught her hands, jerking them up over her head. *"Stop."*

As he lifted his head, their gazes locked and he stared down at her, stroked a hand down, lightly rubbed the heel of his palm against her mound. *"Don't worry...I have plans to do this many times tonight,"* he told her.

Then he stopped touching her long enough to shove his pants down one-handed.

With her arms still pinned overhead, she was trapped, helpless...unable to do anything but wait.

Her breath hitched in her chest as he leaned into her, pale blue eyes glittering with heat and desire. He caught one leg, guided it over his hip. *"Wrap your legs around me,"* he ordered.

Vanya brought her other leg up, whimpered as the position opened her, had her pressed against him—open, wet, waiting...vulnerable.

His gaze captured hers, held it.

And then he pushed forward.

Vanya's lashes fluttered down.

"No—"

His voice was a harsh demand in her head—velvet rasping inside her skull, demanding, seductive.

"Look at me..."

Groaning, Vanya forced her lashes up, stared at him. Watched him as he slowly, oh so slowly sank inside her.

The thickness of his cock throbbed, pulsed, lodged just inside her pussy. Inch by slow inch, he sank inside.

She arched forward, whimpering as he stretched her.

Silence dipped his head, rubbed his lips over her mouth. Soft, slow kisses, teasing and sweet. He slipped a hand between them, his thumb unerringly seeking out the tight bud of her clit, stroking it. She gasped out his name, jerked against his hold, desperate to wrap her arms around him—to feel all of him.

Not just his body, and not just his voice rumbling inside her head...

"Open for me, Vanya...open...sweet, so damn sweet..."

Although, damn, she did like the sound of his voice rumbling inside her head.

Tearing her mouth from his, she jerked against his hold again and said, "Let go of my hands."

Slowly, his fingers uncurled, stroked down her arms.

She wound her arms around his neck, fisted her hands in the golden silk of his hair. Staring into his eyes, she tugged his mouth back to hers. One hand, big and scarred, came up, framed her face, held her as he lightly kissed her. A butterfly kiss…so light, so gentle.

She pressed her nails into his scalp, whispered against his lips, "Kiss me, damn it."

He grinned against her mouth.

Then, without pause, Silence slanted his mouth over hers, kissing her—his tongue twining with hers, stroking, teasing. Sharing heat and promises…so deep, so hot. It was almost a seduction in itself, that kiss, so intimate and intense.

He stroked his hand down, cupped her hips, held her steady as he started to rock slowly, moving in a circular, teasing angle—the head of his cock hitting her just so—

Oh, hell… Vanya sobbed into his mouth, felt the burn spread through her, felt the need blister inside. His cock swelled. His mouth devoured hers—she felt surrounded by him—felt lost in him.

Unable to breathe, unable to see, she tore her mouth away and cried out his name.

"Yes…" His voice was a demanding, harsh growl in her mind, and it left her burning even hotter, even more hungry.

The hand he had between them, that diabolical hand, continued to toy with her clit, stroking, teasing, rubbing.

Vanya felt the orgasm gathering, tightening—felt *him*, like he was taking her over. Too much, too much—and when she closed her eyes, Silence pulled his hand, stopped touching her, stopped stroking her to reach up and cup her face. "*Look at me,*" he demanded.

Too much, she thought, thankful he couldn't hear *her* thoughts...

But he could see. She suspected. If she looked at him, he'd see how shaken she was. How much she needed this, how much she wanted *him*...not just sex, but *him*...this man she barely knew.

No...

His hand fisted in her hair, tugged. The pale, ice-blue of his eyes filled her vision. *Look at me*—his voice was now a snarl in her mind, his mouth so close, so close...

"I want to see you, Vanya."

Had to see her...had to watch those dark eyes as they went near black as she came ever closer to coming, had to see the pleasure, and even the nerves, although why she was nervous...

Gentling his hands, he stroked down, cupped her hips. Easing back, he reached out to her mind, still amazed that he'd found somebody who he could *speak* to, somebody who could *hear* him. "Look at us, if you cannot look at me. Watch..."

Her eyes darted to his then away. Away...dropping down to linger where he entered her, his paler curls tangling with her darker ones, the pink lips of her sex stretching around his cock, his flesh slick with her arousal.

"*So pretty...*"

She whimpered.

Looking up, he stared into her eyes. Saw the heat burning there. The hunger.

The need...and yes, the nerves.

For reasons he didn't understand, it made his heart clench. Cuddling her close, he pulled away from the window, carried her to the closest bed, so miserable and hard. He wanted one as soft as a cloud for this. He lay down, pulled her atop him, but when she went to sit up, he kept her cuddled close, taking her mouth with his. *Sweet...*

Her tongue stroked over his, her mouth moving soft and certain.

Sweet, he thought again as she started to rock, the slick, satiny walls of her pussy tight and hot.

He cupped her ass, arched up to meet her.

Shuddering as she pressed down harder, moved faster.

Closer now, so damn close...

Her teeth sank into his lip. Her nails bit into his skin.

Then she tore her mouth away and screamed his name.

As she came around him, he rolled and put her under him.

Dimly, he thought he should try to silence her broken cries...

But it was the sweetest damn sound...

Burying his face against her neck, he sank into her, hard, deep...and when the climax hit him, blindingly sweet, he only wished he could have told her—in true words—how fucking good she felt.

He might have tried to tell her anyway, except there was a knock at the door.

Vanya groaned and shoved against his chest. "The damn food," she muttered.

For a moment, he was tempted to ignore it. Then he felt guilty...she needed the food, needed to rest.

Sighing, he pulled out and rolled away, watching as she climbed to her feet and grabbed a sheet to wrap around herself.

A smile curled his lips as he imagined peeling that sheet away.

After she'd eaten, of course.

Morning came.

She would have ignored it, but she was miserably uncomfortable, and when she went to shift on the bed, one eye absently popping open, it occurred to her that the other bed looked a little too high and the ceiling looked farther away than it should.

Frowning, she pushed up onto her elbow and stared at the floor.

That was when she saw Silence was already awake and watching her.

He didn't seem to sleep as much as she did, she'd already noticed.

When she'd asked him, he'd told her that once she'd adjusted, she'd only *want* rest for a few hours a day and she could actually go without it for a week or more if necessary.

He was smiling at her, one hand toying with her short, tousled curls.

She blushed, even though she didn't know why.

"Good morning," he murmured inside her head.

"Hi."

She glanced around again, once more staring at the floor. Squirming around, she sat up and then peered over the edge of the bed, her eyes flying wide open as she saw the remains of the bed frame. "Um...Silence...we broke the bed."

The bed shook a little, and when she look back at him, he was laughing—that soundless laughter.

Her heart ached at the sight.

Damn it.

This was bad.

She wasn't supposed to fall for him, she knew.

But she was.

Covering her worry with a scowl, she muttered, "Yeah, you laugh. You're not the one who's down to about two hundred dollars."

He stroked a hand down her back, guided her back against him.

"I'll take care of the bed...after all, I probably broke it."

"How do you know?"

There was a pause, and in the back of her mind, she could hear the hum of his thoughts. Then he replied, *"I weigh more. It makes sense. Besides, it's my bed."*

"Good point."

He started toying with her hair again. *"You wore a wig that first night."*

"Yeah. Throw off how I look. I don't suppose you know where it is, do you?"

"I have it. It's been cleaned. But I like your curls." There was a strange note in his mental voice, one she couldn't place. *"Why wear it?"*

It did another one of those weird numbers to her heart too.

"Eh, it's just a disguise thing. Between the curls and my scars..." She absently reached up to touch them.

He caught her wrist, tugging her hand away and replacing her fingers with his lips. *"Those scars are nothing—nothing for you to hide, nothing for you to be ashamed of."*

She blushed. Lowering her gaze, she cuddled against him and pressed her face against his chest. "It's not a hiding thing so much. I've gotten used to the scars...mostly. It's just between the curls and the scars, I stand out. I can't afford to do that—the last thing I need is to be remembered and get in trouble.

"Although..." She smiled and looked up at him. "Maybe I won't need it now. You're supposed to show me how to stay out of trouble, right?"

"Yes. Except I get the feeling you're going to be more trouble than I planned, Vanya."

She laughed. "Sorry."

"I'm not."

Chapter Five

This was a part of her training Vanya hadn't been prepared for, not at all.

Of course, the past few months of her life had been nothing but one change after another, so maybe she should stop trying to prepare for anything.

But this...

Whoa...

In the pit of her belly, there was a hot ball of hunger, mixed with more than a little shame, a healthy dose of embarrassment.

Right across from them, set up on one of the "stages", Vanya was watching two people go at it.

They were human, at least—most of the people in this club *were* human. Her skin didn't have that nasty buzz she always got when there were too many of the demonic around.

It would so much worse if she was getting off watching a demon screw a human—hell, she didn't know if she could have just *sat* there for that. Especially not with the succubae or incubae—sex was food to them.

Squirming, Vanya crossed her legs and clenched her thighs together, wished that would help. Silence stood behind her, but he didn't seem as enraptured as she was. She *wanted* to look away, but she couldn't. Silence didn't have that problem. The look on his face was one of sheer boredom, and she could tell by the tone of his thoughts, he wasn't particularly overtaken by lust.

Unlike her...

She swallowed, staring at the scene in front of her, wishing she could look away but utterly unable to do so.

The man held the woman restrained against the wall, facing away from him as he took her from behind.

If Vanya hadn't watched the woman lead him to the stage, hadn't seen an odd moment of tenderness between them before they'd gotten started, she might have been worried—or outright pissed—and then she would have been storming the stage. From everything she could *see*, the woman was struggling. He held her restrained, used his body to overpower her...to force her.

If it had been true force, Vanya knew she wouldn't have felt this way—she'd seen enough of *that* shit to know. So why did she feel so turned on watching this...pretense?

Was it because she could see the woman's excitement?

Because she had even *seen* it, glimpsed inside the woman's mind? She'd been freaked out when she'd first seen what was happening, and instinctively, she'd lowered her shields—and what she'd read from the woman was *not* fear.

A hand touched her arm and she jumped, looked up to see Silence staring down at her.

She blushed hotly.

"If you wish, we can leave until they are done," he offered. *"This disturbs many people."*

Part of her thought that was exactly what they needed to do—and she *was* disturbed...just not the way she *should* be, she suspected. But she gave him what she hoped was a nonchalant smile. "No. I'm fine."

Fine...hot, horny...would you please do that to me? She tore her gaze from him before he saw that on her face. The last thing she needed for him to see just then was that she was discovering some latent kinky streak—one centering on some hot, wanton desire involving mock-force, rape fantasy and Silence.

But is it really latent? I mean, I've had some rough, kinky sex fantasies... just not quite this *rough...*

And never in so much detail—

Good thing, because she might not have been withstood the shock of it.

Her entire body was hot, aching, and between her thighs, she was one, giant throbbing need.

Staring at the stage, she watched as the man pulled away and turned his partner around. The woman pretended to jerk back—or at least try to. He didn't let her, forcing her to the floor and coming down on top of her—she struggled, harder and harder—From here, Vanya could hear her moans, and she echoed them in her mind.

"It's not real."

Vanya shot Silence a look. "What?"

"It's not real—she wants this," he said, nodding toward the stage.

"I know," she said, swallowing.

"You..." Abruptly his eyes narrowed.

Oh, hell, she must have made some sound, something that made Silence think she was freaking out. Well, she was, but not for the reasons he thought. Blushing furiously, she tore her eyes from him. "I know it's not real," she said stiffly. She went to turn around on her barstool.

She felt the warmth of his amusement...and something deeper, darker wash over her as he moved to stand behind her. His hands came to rest on her shoulders, forcing her back around to watch the couple. *"Watch if you wish...that's why they are there. It's not like they care...they want to be watched."*

She still burned with embarrassment, but with Silence standing behind her, if she turned around, she'd be on face level with his chest. His hands stroked down her shoulders, up, the tips of his fingers almost reaching the tops of her breasts.

The man had the woman's wrists pinned over her head now. Her back arched. Vanya almost expected to see her legs spread wide, but they weren't. The man was thrusting into her, fighting against her clenched thighs—it would be tighter that way—harder...

Vanya whimpered.

Unable to watch anymore, she scooted off the stool. Her legs wobbled underneath her and she thought she might fall down, but then Silence was there, one hand under her elbow, holding her steady.

She might have thought to question where he was taking her, what he was doing, but she didn't even know where she'd been planning on going. And what did it matter...

She didn't know where he took her—her heart was pounding so hard against her ribs, her breathing hard and fast. One moment they were in the middle of the raucous sex club, surrounded by loud, driving music, and then it was dark, quiet...

Too dark... His shadows.

What...

She might have asked, but his mouth was on hers and his hand was between her thighs— She clenched her legs against his entry, resisting him, even as she welcomed it.

She cried out as he drove two thick, long fingers into her aching sex, twisted them. *"That's my girl..."*

The rough velvet of his voice crowded her mind, his body surrounded hers. He pressed his thumb against her clit, rotated it around the stiff little nub. *"Your heart is racing,"* he murmured. His free hand rested on her neck, and under it, she could feel the thrum of her pulse. *"You're so hot, you burn, Vanya. You burn me."*

She clung to him, clenched her legs as he worked his fingers inside her.

"You feel tighter that way. I'd like to be inside you right now...What you saw excited you, didn't it?"

She gasped as he lifted his head and stared down at her.

"Answer me..."

"Yes," she whimpered, shuddering as he ground the heel of his palm against her clit, a harsh cry rising. She bit her lip to hold it back, but he caught her mouth again, swallowing the sound down.

"Would you like me to do that you?"

Her knees went weak, and if he hadn't held her, she might have collapsed as she thought of it, thought of him pushing her skirt up, pushing her up against the wall—taking her, fast, hard, her hands restrained, his body overpowering hers—

Even as the image formed in her mind, the need swelled to a crescendo, and just like that, she came.

"You're beautiful," he murmured, pressing his lips to her brow, stroking her back as her breathing slowed.

Vanya squirmed and shook her head.

"No, I'm not." She might not be utterly hideous, but any chance she'd had at true beauty had died a few years ago. The scars on her face saw to that. Although she hadn't thought about them lately—Silence didn't even seem to notice them.

"Don't you think I should be the one who decides?"

He was smiling, she could tell. *"If I think you're beautiful, then to me, you are beautiful."* He kissed her gently, his voice a whisper in her mind, *"And, Vanya, you are beautiful."*

Sighing, she slipped her arms around his waist. "You're good on a girl's ego, you know that?"

Good on the ego. Bad on the heart. But she wasn't going to worry about that now.

Tipping her head back, she smiled at him. "Well, now that you've gotten my mind…ah…settled, maybe we should go out there and do what we came to do?"

He grinned at her.

"Yes. Then we can leave and you can help me settle my mind…*and then you can answer my question."*

"Your question?" She stared at him, confused.

He gripped the hem of her skirt, drawing it up slowly, his face stark, almost harsh. *"What you saw…would you like me to do that to you?"*

Vanya gulped. "Ah…hell. I…" She licked her lips. "I don't know. I…just don't know. I think I would, but…"

He kissed her, hard, almost too hard, but it had that same knee-buckling effect. *"If you decide…"* He let her skirt go, and then turned her around, nudged her forward. *"But for now, we have a job to do."*

I'm such a tramp. A hopeless, lovesick tramp.

Almost an hour had passed. She was back on a barstool. Alone.

Not for long, though.

Morosely, Vanya watched as Silence walked across the bar's dance floor.

Here she was in the middle of a sex club, her body still buzzing from the arousal from earlier. In the back of her mind, she was aware of a discordant cadence—succubae, incubae...demons. They'd have to deal with them tonight—after all, that was *why* they were here, to see how she could handle one on her own now that she was one of the Grimm.

But all she could think was, *Damn, he looks hot, and if those bitches don't quit staring at him, I'm going to hurt them.*

Some of those bitches were demons.

But most of them were human, and hell, she couldn't *blame* them for staring at Silence.

He was damn well worth staring at. He was so damned beautiful—angelically beautiful, even. She smirked as she thought it. Then she thought about what he'd said, what he'd offered.

That dark, disturbing fantasy.

Her belly turned into a hot, nervous tangle and she needed a drink even thinking about it.

"The job," she told herself. "Think about the damn job."

It wasn't like that wasn't enough to keep her mind occupied right now.

She was getting ready to actually engage with the enemy.

She'd been moved from the basic part of training to the actual fighting-with-demons part.

He hadn't given it a fancy name—just told her a week ago she'd be engaging with demons soon.

After two months of being pummeled by him during the nights and spending the dawn hours under him and a few hours of the day wrapped around him, she was moving from punching bag to demon fodder.

Yay.

Of course, he hadn't told her she was going to be demon fodder.

She just *felt* that way.

There were more demons here than she was used to dealing with. She could feel them. Feel them in a way she hadn't felt them before. She'd all but started shaking when he'd led her in here, and only his hand on her back had kept her from bolting.

His hand…and the low, soothing rumble of his voice in her mind. *You'll be fine. This is nothing you haven't done before, remember that. You've fought succubae and incubae—when you were human, and you did fine. You are ready for this. I wouldn't bring you here if you weren't ready, and I'll never be too far from your side, I promise.*

He'd kept that promise too.

Save for when he left to get her a drink, he'd hardly left her side at all.

They'd danced, they'd necked in the corner, they'd watched the couple act out a rape fantasy, and then he'd used his very talented hands to give her several delightful orgasms.

And now…

He was coming back to her with a glint in his eye and a man in tow.

Except the man behind him wasn't a man.

It was an incubae, and Vanya knew she'd dealt with his kind before—there was no reason to be so scared—*none*. She'd killed these things before, on her own, and she wasn't alone now.

But something felt...different. Off.

Hell. Maybe it was just her.

She'd been on edge ever since she'd stepped into the club, and it wasn't just because she'd watched the hottest damn sexual act ever, and it wasn't just from what Silence had offered.

Nerves, she told herself. Just nerves and she needed to get *over* it.

Now. Because the incubae was only five feet away and he was staring at her like she was a piece of candy and he was starving for a taste.

Demon...

Vanya saw it in his eyes.

"He thinks we're looking for a third," Silence said to her. *"And he already thinks you're nervous, so we don't need to worry about that."*

Briefly she wondered how he'd managed to communicate with the guy, but five seconds later, she figured it out.

The guy was already trying to crawl all over her, his hands coming to rest on her outer thighs while he nuzzled her neck. "Fuck, you're hot. I've been watching you two since you came in, baby, and I've been hoping you were looking for some more action. Lucky me..."

Obviously Silence hadn't needed to speak—the man had done all the speaking for him.

She stared over his shoulder at Silence, well aware that her eyes were too wide, that she probably looked a little too panicked. Damn it, she couldn't do this—couldn't do it...

A hand touched her shoulder. Warm, hard, scarred—she knew that touch. Turning her head, she stared into Silence's blue eyes. He cupped her chin, angled her head back. As his mouth covered hers, he murmured into her mind, *"He can't stop talking any easier than I can talk, it seems. Relax...he's new, unused to being in the mortal world, I suspect. All we need to do is get him outside. He already thinks I've talked you into this, so that's why you're nervous."*

Nervous?

Shit.

Vanya wasn't nervous.

She was *terrified*.

The man currently rubbing his crotch against her leg was a *demon*. She was used to demons, yeah. But she wasn't used to being quite so surrounded by them, and Silence had already told her they were going to do the kill *here*—not away from the rest of the others, but *here*. And if more came, she was supposed to deal with it.

Deal with more than a couple of them at a time.

His tongue teased her lips, and his voice, that teasing, rough rumble in her mind said, *"Open for me...relax. Ah, you're sweet, Vanya..."*

The ridged scars on his palms rasped over her flesh as he stroked a hand up over her arm, her shoulder, cupping her neck.

"Y'all want go into the back? Find one of the rooms?" their new companion asked, right when she'd thought *maybe* she could relax.

This was better, though.

Because the sooner they got moving, the sooner she could either try to kill this guy or screw up so Silence could step in.

And shit, how pathetic was that? She'd killed these things before. A lot. Without Silence's help, on her own, back when she'd been a human. Just because she'd lured them away and acted on a one-on-one or two-on-one basis didn't change things much.

She was more than human now.

She could handle this.

Pulling her mouth away from Silence, she looked at the incubae.

Well, he was a good-looking bastard, she'd give him that.

They usually were, though.

His eyes ran over her with appreciation, never once pausing at her scarred face. No, he was too interested in staring at her tits, which were very much on display in the corset she wore in lieu of a top. That and a microscopic skirt consisted of her clothing. The boots covered more flesh than the skirt did, for crying out loud, coming up to her knees. Fortunately, there was no heel to the boot, and she knew she'd be able to move in them—she'd already checked that out.

She also had her knives stashed inside them.

Suddenly, eager hands were gripping her waist, pulling her from the stool where she was sitting. Realizing the guy had taken her silence for consent, she stiffened.

"We need him outside," Silence said into her mind, his voice hard and flat. *"I will not risk you getting cornered with this many of the possessed. You're too new."*

Even as he said it, he slipped an arm around her waist, nuzzling her neck—maybe to look as though he were encouraging her.

Stiffening her legs, she gave the demon tugging on her hand a nervous look and shook her head. "How about outside?"

she shouted, raising her voice, even though she knew she didn't need to.

She leaned against Silence, not having to feign her nervousness or the shyness as the guy looked at her. The indulgent smile curling his lips made her want to pop him, though.

Silence's hand, resting on her waist, tightened. *"Breathe, dear one...don't let him know you're angered. He can sense it as well as I can."*

Turning her face into Silence's chest, she took a deep, steady breath, forced the tight muscles in her back to relax. Then she pushed back and gave Silence a tight smile. She couldn't get rid of the anger altogether, or the nervousness. Rising up on her toes, she curled a hand around his neck and tugged him down. She didn't have to talk loud—the demon would hear her, and that was the point. "Do you have any idea just how *big* you're going to owe me for this, baby? Sooooo big. I'm thinking oral sex and breakfast in bed every day for a month."

As she settled back down in front of him, Silence flashed her a wide grin, and in her mind, she felt the warm blast of approval.

No, she couldn't hide her discomfort. Might as well roll with it, right?

As the demon came up behind her and started to rub his cock against her ass, she clenched her jaw.

Silence caught her face in his hands just as the demon cupped her breasts and teased, "Come on, angel...relax. You got no idea how much fun we can show you."

She blushed a brilliant shade of red, shooting a look around the club. Yeah, people were looking at them, but it wasn't in shock.

Hell, it was a fucking *sex* club.

Of course people were looking at them.

But she had to get away from their stares before she cracked.

"Take me outside," she said, her voice strained even to her own ears.

Silence tugged her away from the other man, his arm curling around her. Tucked against his leather-clad side, she relaxed a little, even as the demon came up next to them, his hand settling low on her back, his fingers toying with the laces of her corset.

"You're doing fine," Silence assured her as they broke through the crowd.

Out in the cool darkness of the evening, she managed, finally, to breathe. The itching, tight sensation along her spine relaxed and she let him guide them around the building. He'd already scoped it out, picked out the exact area he wanted to use.

Smart, prepared...so much more equipped to handle this than she was.

Damn it, was what she doing—

A hand clamped over her ass.

She stiffened but managed not to pull away. Barely. Just barely.

In the darkness, Silence came to a stop.

They were at the very far edges of the parking lot where, handily, lights were out. Handily—she'd watched as he took care of them. Not too many mortals would come to this area because of the darkness, and as she leaned against him, she watched as the darkness thickened.

"Dude, it's fucking dark over here," the demon muttered, his voice oddly strained. "Why not go back inside, beautiful? I want to see that pretty mouth of yours..."

"He's used to being able to see in the dark and he can't see past my illusions," Silence said. Because she was touching him, the shadows weren't affecting her and she could see the way the other guy's dark eyes were darting around nervously.

Swallowing, she stepped away from Silence, relying on her ears to guide her to the other man, because once she wasn't *touching* Silence, the darkness was complete, like being wrapped in black cotton and thrown in a cave with no exit, no natural light, nothing.

She could hear him, faintly.

Reaching out, she touched him. Her fingers brushed against a hard, flat stomach. Trailing them lower, she curled her hand around the front of his leather pants, tugged him forward. "I like it better out here," she said softly. "It's quieter...and I'm already nervous. Besides..." she had to force the breathy little giggle, but it sounded legit enough. "I've got a thing for doing it outside."

The incubae relaxed as she touched him, giving in to the nature that ruled him. His mouth came down, finding hers easily enough, despite the dark. "Do you, angel?"

Angel—

She coyly tugged her head aside, guided his mouth to her neck and wiggled around in his arms so that she was facing Silence again.

Knowing he'd see her, even if she couldn't see him, she signed, *Now?*

"It's your move, Vanya. I'm just the backup."

Behind her, the demon was rocking against her. She felt his cock nudging her backside.

She hissed as something hot, thick, insidious rolled through the air. She hadn't felt anything quite like that before. It was...unreal. Wrong. And it made her so fucking hot. As he pumped his hips against her scantily covered butt, she found, to her horror, she was getting turned on. Heat coursed through her, stealing her breath and turning everything inside her to hot, molten liquid.

As he slid a hand around her waist and up the front of her skirt, she shuddered, cried out. And horrified delight hurtled through her when he touched her—

Heat...hunger...devastatingly powerful...

She had to...

No— Sucking in a breath, she closed her eyes, realized what was happening. She was standing there. Letting this...*thing*...this parasite, this *killer* touch her. And she was *enjoying* it—even craving it.

Oh, no—

She reached down into her boot, grabbed her knife.

Then she whirled.

Without thinking or planning.

She couldn't even see him—

And then she could, just in time to realize now he could see her because Silence had dropped the shadows.

The demon could see her, and the knife.

He snarled, but it was too late. She'd already buried it in his heart.

The heart that was still human, even if the demon controlled the body.

As easily as that, he was dead.

Shuddering, shaking from the effects of whatever had her turned her on, she turned around and demanded, "What in the hell was that?"

Silence was staring at her, his blue eyes cold.

Pissed.

She didn't *care*.

"What in the *hell* was that?"

His hands slashed through the air. "*That was you almost getting fucked—and I'm not talking about sex, Vanya, although I didn't expect to see you letting him go so far. You didn't think at all.*"

Sputtering, the bloody knife still clutched in her hand, she stared at him. "I didn't *think*? Um, excuse me, I've killed more of these things than I can remember and I've never felt anything like that—what in the hell was that?"

She felt a blast of cold in her mind, and although that nasty, clinging residue of unwanted arousal lingered, it was no longer the driving force in her mind. Now she was awash in Silence's anger, the knife edge of an icy rage. And all it did was make her even more pissed.

Distantly, she heard the chaos in his mind—the way she did when he was either thinking random thoughts or trying to block her. Damn it, he'd better be blocking because right now she was so fucking pissed, if she heard him too clearly, they'd be going at it.

Shaking with her own anger, trembling with fear and disgust, she said, "Again, what in the *hell* was that?"

His hands flashed, moving too quick for her to follow.

"Damn it, either slow down or just *talk* to me," she snarled.

His eyes narrowed. Then his hand moved, again too fast. But he wasn't signing to her this time. This time, he was grabbing her, his hand hooking in the front of her corset and hauling her against him.

His face just a breath from hers, he glared at her. The look on his face was one of sheer, icy rage. *"Just talk to you, Vanya? How can I just talk when you threw everything I've taught you out the window and reacted blindly?"*

"Damn it, I was freaked out! I still am, and you haven't answered me—what in the hell was that? Why in the hell did I suddenly *want* him touching me?"

A muscle ticked in Silence's jaw.

She shuddered at the rage she felt coming from him, rage, worry, jealousy...confusion.

Then he closed his eyes.

His hand uncurled from her corset and she was able to sink back to her feet, still watching him, still confused as all get out.

She went to push her hair back from her face and saw she was still holding the knife. "Fuck," she muttered, her voice cracking a little. She wanted to cry. Wanted to curl up into a ball and sob. And she also itched, ached with the need to fuck—her entire body burned with it. Swallowing past the knot in her throat, she shoved it all aside. She wasn't done here, after all, right?

She sank to the ground, unable to exactly *bend*—not in the corset. She used the dead guy's shirt to clean her knife, eying his face.

He was just a dead body now—a dead man.

A human.

One she'd killed.

Sighing, she whispered to him, "I'm sorry."

Silence touched her head. *"You know you had no choice. Once an incubae settles in, we cannot get them out. If he'd fought, there might have been a chance, but he wasn't fighting. You could see the demon in control, couldn't you?"*

She eased away, shaken, still angry, so confused. Not to mention hurt and scared. She moved until he couldn't touch her and shot a nervous look around the parking lot. Tucking her knife back into her boot, she said, "We've been out here too long. We're going to be seen."

Silence shook his head. *"No—"*

Then, abruptly, he stopped speaking and signed. *I'm hiding this area. Nobody can see us or hear us. For all the world knows, this area doesn't exist right now.*

He lifted a hand as though to touch her.

Vanya backed away even as her belly went hot and tight, even as her nipples drew tight.

What the *hell*—? She crossed her arms over her chest, but that was almost agony.

"Damn it, why am I feeling like this, damn it?" she demanded, humiliated when her voice broke. "I've been around those things too many times and I've had them pawing me too. But I've never been turned on by one. I never *wanted* one."

Silence sighed, the soft sound breaking the quiet that wrapped around them. His hand, still stretched out between them, curled into a fist and then fell to his side.

She stared at him, waiting for an answer.

When he spoke into her mind, she jumped.

"It may be that you'd always shielded against it. But it's just the power of their kind, Vanya. It's nothing unusual. I've felt it myself—and it's nothing for you to feel shame over. You didn't

want *him. It was your body reacting without your consent to something he did—you can't be blamed for blinking, for breathing. It was an instinctive response, nothing to feel ashamed over, nothing to be angry over."*

Then he passed a hand over his face, shook his head. *"Your powers have increased with your change—they often do. It never occurred to me that you were unfamiliar with what they can do since you've fought them before. If you'd had a natural resistance to them as a mortal, I would have thought it would carry over."*

He looked at her, his blue eyes troubled. He lifted his hands and signed.

I'm sorry.

Vanya swallowed and looked away.

Shit.

He was sorry—for what? Still squirming, still miserable, still fighting her own anger, she looked away. Her voice stiff, she said, "You expected me to think and I didn't. You've been training me to think and I didn't. I fucked up, for whatever reasons. Don't be sorry. I'll do better next time."

She went to brush past him. His hand came down over her neck and squeezed.

"You had a right to be disturbed by that—I would have been if I hadn't been expecting it." His thumb and fingers lightly dug into the tight muscles, coaxing them into relaxing.

Vanya didn't want to relax, though.

She couldn't, not until she figured out a way to function with this shit.

Hell, she'd blocked the things before—shielded against it, a natural resistance, whatever. She'd figure it out again. "Disturbed or not, I'm supposed to think, right?" She moved away from his hand, heading toward the club. The farther she moved away, the louder the music got, the brighter the parking lot got.

"We're done for the night," he said a few moments later.

She briefly wondered what had become of the body, or if it was still lying back there.

"We're not done," she said. "You told me I had to do this a couple of times, damn it. I'm doing it a couple of times."

She'd be damned if she let these things freak her out so badly that she couldn't function—hell, she'd done better as a human.

That wasn't acceptable.

"Damn it, stop being so stubborn," Silence snapped, reaching for her.

But she evaded him, her body swaying to the side only a second before he would have closed his hand around her shoulder. That smooth, white shoulder left bare by the corset he'd provided for her to wear—what had he been thinking?

"I'm not being stubborn," she replied. "I'm doing what you brought me here for, remember? And I'll handle it better this time."

She was still upset. He could see it in the tense set of her shoulders, in the pale, tight look around her eyes.

He wouldn't risk this—

Somebody came around the corner.

A lithe, leggy blonde who took a look at him then Vanya. He recognized her about the same time Vanya did—saw the thing peering out from behind her eyes.

Vanya tripped. On purpose, he was sure, falling against the woman with a soft sob.

"Oh, shit. I'm sorry." She gave a very convincing, completely *fake* sniff and shot him a dirty look. "Would you leave me *alone*? I told you, I'm *not* leaving. You wanted to come here—fine, we're here. Asshole."

She went to go around the blonde, but the woman caught her around the waist. "Are you okay, sweetie?" She shot Silence a smirk and added, "Let me guess. Your boyfriend here doesn't want you having any fun, huh?"

Vanya curled her lip. "Only *his* kind of fun, the bastard." She tried to push away from the blonde, subtly, putting some distance between them.

"Hmmm. Typical man." She stroked a hand down Vanya's arm.

Silence felt the prickle of her power roll through the air.

It was stronger than the incubae had been, and if he could speak, he would have sworn a blue streak. As it was, he was hard-pressed not to blast his voice in Vanya's mind, knowing she'd be getting the full brunt of the succubae's power, completely unprepared, and touching the demon as well.

"What's he wanting, sweetie? The typical male-pig thing? Having two women crawling all over him?" She inched closer. Her eyes were darker now, the demon inching closer and closer to the surface.

Vanya swayed forward. "Um. No. He wanted..." She looked away, shot Silence another dark look. "Another guy. Wanted me to do it with another guy. And him. I didn't want to—the other guy got mad and I...hell, I hit him. I think I broke his nose and he got mad, took off."

Clever girl, Silence thought. That would explain any blood the succubae might scent on her if she stopped thinking with her cunt long enough.

"Broke his nose, did you? And you still want to stay?"

Vanya poked her lip out. "I want a drink. I want to dance. And...hell. I don't know. I want to have some fun, but I don't think I want to be with two guys. He won't shut up about it and now he's pouting."

"Hmmmm...that sounds like a man. And two men, well, it can be fun. But still, you should get to choose your own games," the blonde whispered. She had a hand on Vanya's waist now, stroking upward to her breasts.

Vanya blushed when the blonde touched her. Blushed, shivered, turned away. "I...um..."

The blonde touched her mouth to Vanya's shoulder. Silence watched, set his jaw. And called his shadows, wrapping them around them. As he did, he eased closer to Vanya, reaching out to touch her, his fingers brushing the tips of hers as he lowered his mouth to hers.

The succubae chuckled. "Well, maybe two women will work for him as well, sweetie. I think he just wants to see you having fun, really...look at how he looks at you. He's completely gone over on you, I can tell."

Silence stroked his hand down her torso. The succubae had slid her hands around, dipped them inside the top of Vanya's corset to toy with her breasts.

Silence could feel her touching his woman and it bothered him—he'd played this game and it had never affected him before. It was an easy way to set up this kind of demon—they were so easily distracted with the lure of sex, all save the king or queen.

But he hated this because he could see the discomfort in Vanya's eyes. Even under the impact of the succubae's power, she was still herself—and she didn't like this, at all. It infuriated him.

Stroking his hand farther down, he trailed his fingers over her thigh, catching her knee, bringing it up.

A few seconds later, he had her knife in his hand.

Vanya tensed as the succubae screeched.

Her scream ended abruptly, and Vanya jerked out from the little demon/angel sandwich she'd been in.

Staring at Silence, staring at the knife he held, she set her jaw.

"Damn it, am I supposed to be learning or not?" she demanded.

"Yes. But I'm not putting more on you than you need, and you've done enough tonight." He cleaned the blade and handed it back to her. She took it, about ready to spin around, heading back into the club. But he caught her arm, his grasp too tight to break.

As he hustled her toward the car, she snapped, "Damn it, we can't just leave. What about the bodies?"

He smirked. *"We leave them. You've done that before, I know."*

Vanya winced. Yeah, there were a number of cops who really wanted her ass—hell, they'd probably branded her a serial killer. "I thought you all operated with a little more polish. Besides, this place has cameras. I saw them."

A grim smile twisted his mouth. *"Cameras don't like me. The security people will find them all broken. Another gift of mine. Stop dragging your feet, Vanya. We are leaving."*

They reached the car far too soon, but before she could climb in, he touched her cheek. *"You are still unhappy with me."*

She gave him a flat look. "I've had a bad night. And since we're not staying, can we just *go*? I want a damn bath."

He sighed and dipped his head, brushing his lips over her brow. Then he stepped back, letting her climb in. The door closed behind her and she closed her eyes. She wanted a bath, and despite the fact that she wasn't supposed to *need* sleep, she did. She actually kind of craved it, needed the oblivion it promised.

Chapter Six

"Why are we here?" Vanya sighed as Silence parked the car in front of a luxury hotel that she'd seen before, but damned if she had ever so much as stepped a foot inside.

She couldn't afford this place.

She probably couldn't even afford the *soap* in this place.

"I'm tired of that hovel. We're moving to this hotel."

She stiffened. "That *hovel* is where I've been living for several months. If it doesn't suit you? Fine. Take me there and you can check your fancy ass into whatever hotel you like."

Silence shot her a narrow look and shook his head.

"Fine," she bit off. "I'll fucking walk."

She was so damned tired it wasn't even funny. Tired, and more than a little embarrassed. Yeah, she knew the rundown little place wasn't much, but hell, it was the best she could manage.

But when she went to get out, Silence's hand closed over her wrist. *"You are not leaving. You do not need to be alone, and you damn well deserve better than that miserable room."*

Flushing a miserable shade of red, she fought the urge to hunch her shoulders.

"That miserable room suits me fine," she bit off.

He snorted. The look on his face said more than enough. *"You're not going back there."*

"My *clothes* are back there. My *money*. Every damn thing I own. And excuse me, but you don't *own* me, do you?" Jerking against his hold, she tried to pull away, but she couldn't. That just pissed her off even more.

Damn it, this night had *sucked.*

Her skin was still prickly tight with the remnants of that awful arousal she'd felt from the incubae then the succubae, although it hadn't been as strong with the succubae. The female demon's power had been stronger, but Vanya had worked harder to shield against it, and she hoped that had helped—maybe that was the key, just a little extra shielding.

She hoped so, because it was the one bright note she had to hold on to.

Glaring at Silence, she snarled, "Let me *go*, damn it. I want to go to my own room, not be bossed around by some commandeering, thoughtless bastard who doesn't give a flying fuck about what I want or what I feel—"

"Is that what you think? You little—"

Then he cut his thoughts off, closed his eyes. Wide shoulders rose and fell as he took a deep breath before looking back at her. Slowly, his fingers uncurled from her wrist. He let go and she jerked her wrist back, went to climb out of the door, but he warned her, *"You take off right now, I will catch you. Do not make me chase you."*

It wasn't so much the words, but the look in his eyes that kept her in place.

Sinking back against the plush leather of the seat, she waited in sullen silence.

She saw his hands from the corner of her eye, pretended she didn't.

Then she felt terribly small.

He wouldn't speak to her mind when he was angry—it was as though he didn't want her to see the things that would make matters worse. If she wouldn't look at him...

Locked in silence...

Sighing, she looked back at him. "What?" she demanded, not caring that she sounded more than a little bitchy.

Come inside. Please. You've had a bad night and you should have a decent meal, a quiet night, he signed.

Something about the look on his face, in his eyes had her heart softening.

Damn it, she didn't like that he could get under her defenses with so little effort. Especially when she *wanted* to be angry, when she knew she was even a little entitled. She didn't like it that he could get to her so easily...didn't like it at all.

Grouchy, she shot him a look from the corner of her eye and then looked back at the hotel. "I can't afford this place—I can't even afford to split it with you."

He touched her arm as he said into her mind, *"Another thing we should talk about...you're not to be a pauper all your life, Vanya. You actually do get paid for this."*

Okay, now *that* wasn't anything she'd been expecting.

"Um...paid?" She snorted. "And it's drawn on what bank, exactly? Almighty God, Inc? Guardian Angels, LLC?"

He grinned. *"Nothing quite so obvious, dear one. But Will and others have...well, businesses in place. And you'll get money. If it makes you feel better, we can split the cost and you can pay me back once you do start getting paid."*

"And when is that?"

He gave her an enigmatic smile. *"When you get out of training. For now...I'm responsible for you. I guess I should have explained that before now."*

"Responsible for me?" She curled a lip at him. *"I am responsible for me."*

"For your actions, your neck, yes. But by our traditions? I am responsible for your way right now." His hand stroked up her arm, curled over the back of her neck. *"Stop being so stubborn, so proud for one night...let me take care of you...I owe you this after being an ass, at least."*

His fingers dug into the tight tense muscles.

She swallowed and looked back at the hotel.

Hell.

"One night," she muttered. "Yeah, I guess you do owe me that much."

If he'd manipulated her into the hotel, he couldn't feel too bad over it.

He might feel bad tomorrow, when he manipulated her into staying longer. But he wasn't taking her back to that squalid little box of a room, not tonight. Not after...

He closed a hand into a fist, forced the rigid muscles in his back to relax.

She was walking in front of him, her ass swinging in that short, snug skirt.

Too many eyes rested on her as they made their way to the check-in desk. He could see her discomfort rising—*damn it.*

She looked lovely, all that pale, soft flesh, but she was also a walking advertisement for sex and they both knew it. It had been ideal for the club, but not exactly ideal in the luxury hotel, something Silence hadn't even thought of—he'd only thought of getting her someplace *else*, away from the darkness and despair that seemed to be her life.

The lady behind the desk gave her a blank look—professional but dismissive.

Silence narrowed his eyes at her.

If he could have...

But he couldn't.

Each way he turned this night, he was messing up, it seemed.

He signed to Vanya, aware of the hotel employee's gaze lingering on his scarred hands.

Can you check us in?

She gave him a worried look, but he reached into his wallet. She didn't have any identification, he knew. He did, though, and it would pass anybody's scrutiny—after all, Will had arranged for it. He gave her a license and credit card.

She arched a brow and then handed it to the woman behind the counter.

Reaching up, he rested a hand on Vanya's neck.

Alone in a room, that was all he wanted.

And he'd make this miserable night up...

The hotel employee looked at them with a brilliant, beaming smile. "Mr. Marseilles, we were expecting you earlier. We've got your rooms all ready for you."

Silence looked at the woman, lifted a brow.

Vanya blinked. "Waiting for us?"

"Yes. The reservations had you down to arrive today." The woman looked at Vanya, her smile faltering a bit before she steadied it.

Silence sighed and signed to Vanya. *Will.*

Then...

His name was Will.

And he offered the silent prisoner a choice.

"The time is coming when you will have a choice, Eustache."

He curled his lip, sneering at Will. He did not care for that name, whether it was his or not. It reminded him of a time when he'd thought he had found something. When he'd hoped for things. When he'd been betrayed.

But because he was curious, he awkwardly used his hands to form the gestures that Will had been teaching him—that hands could be used to form words, he'd never imagined it. But a way to speak again that didn't involve writing out the words.

What kind of choice?

"A hard one," Will answered bluntly. "Men are coming—men who have learned of you and your secrets. They will come and put another man in your place. It's a man who resembles you so it may not be questioned, at least not for some time."

He smirked and tapped his throat, lifting a brow.

Will looked away. "I do not know if he will speak or not. I do not know all the answers. I just know that this is coming—and it will be dangerous for you. When they come for you, they will try to make you use your gift for them—Louis was foolish and let wine loosen his tongue. They don't entirely believe him, but they want to see you for themselves. It will be your best chance to leave these walls for some time."

There was something Will was not telling him. Secrets. He saw them lurking in those silvery eyes.

"Once you are with these men, you will have to make your own choice."

He shook his head and signed, *I will not be used. I will not use this...this evil for others.*

"It's not evil, son," Will said, sighing. "And I know you will not. Just as I know what will become of you when you refuse."

He reached down and touched Eustache's hands. "They will try to convince you. They will beat you. They will torture you. Eventually, they are going to kill you."

He flinched. Shoving to his feet, he started to pace. As he did, his thoughts spun in dizzying circles. Finally, he stopped and faced Will. Slowly, he signed, *This is the choice you speak of? Either do something I know is wrong or die?*

"No. The choice is this...I can see to it that you die quickly, painlessly—it will end for you before they come. You will be spared what they intend to do, and you will go on to what awaits you beyond this life." Will gave him a reassuring smile. "And I promise you, that's not a bad thing.

"Or..." Will's eyes started to glow. "You can meet your destiny with them. Take what they give you. It will be painful, it will be brutal. And they *will* kill you. When your life is taken, it will be returned. You'll rise anew...and become something more."

He stared at Will and wondered if the man had gone mad.

"There you have it. That is your choice. What do you choose?"

Now...

She managed to keep the question behind her teeth until they'd been escorted to their room. If the bellhop was at all curious about their lack of luggage, he was too good at his job to show it. After he'd unlocked the door for them, Vanya had the impression he'd been about to show them around, but Silence cut that off by pushing some bills into his hand, and in under ten seconds, they were alone in the room.

No—not *room*. *Rooms*.

Hell, it was easily four times the size of the little place where she'd been staying. The large, open sitting area had a wet bar, and she was tempted to go get a drink but too uncomfortable to do so—how much did a drink in this place cost, anyway?

"Okay, how in the hell did *Will* know we were coming here?"

Silence scowled. *"Will knows everything."* Apparently he wasn't so worried about things like how much the drinks cost, though. He was already over at the bar, splashing whiskey into a glass.

She turned away and made her way to the couch, sinking down on it with a sigh. Tired. Too damn tired. The puzzle of Will was just another problem that would have to wait until tomorrow.

She unzipped her boots and tugged them off, sighing with relief as she curled her toes into the plush carpet. Oh, that felt nice. Feeling the weight of his stare, she looked up.

Silence still stood by the bar, drink in hand. His eyes lingered on her legs, but as she looked at him, he looked up, met her gaze.

Swallowing, she looked away. Sensing he was about to say something, she blurted out, "So. Eustache Marseilles, huh? I guess that's not your real name?"

Silence's mouth quirked in a smile. He put his glass down and signed, *We all get the identities we need to move in this* world. You'll get one. Will probably already has one in place for you.

"Hmmm. And I noticed that wasn't an answer." She shrugged. Sliding off the couch, she said, "That's okay. I kind of like Silence better than Eustache anyway. Still, I wouldn't mind knowing your real name."

"I don't know my real name." He turned away from her.

She froze, staring at him. She knew her mouth had fallen open, was vaguely aware that she was staring at him in numb, horrified shock. But she couldn't help it.

Any more than she could help the pain ripping through her.

"You..." She stopped, licked her lips. Tried again. "You don't know your name?"

He looked back over his shoulder at her. With a jerky shrug, he spoke quietly into her mind. *"There is a name I was given at birth, but whatever it was, I've long forgotten it. Eustache Marseilles is simply one of the names I go by when I must give a name. To those who matter, I am simply Silence."*

To those who matter, Vanya thought.

With a tiny smile, she murmured, "So, does that mean I'm one who matters?"

"Of course," he said, his voice soft, quiet.

She started across the carpet, her feet sinking into it.

"After all, you're my student. You matter very much."

Those words slashed across her heart.

She almost stumbled. Almost faltered.

Student... Vanya stilled, staring at him as she repeated that word silently to herself. She was a student. His student.

Yeah, his lover too. But mostly, he just saw her as his student.

His responsibility.

Fuck.

She couldn't do this.

Staring into his pale blue eyes, she swallowed and then looked away. "I want a bath. Then I want to rest. I'm exhausted."

He waited until the door shut quietly behind her.

Then he lifted the glass he held, emptied it and turned, hurled it against the far wall. It shattered, splintered into unrecognizable shards.

Why did I say that...?

Yes. She was his student.

But she was more...his friend, his lover...his everything.

No—he couldn't risk that. He knew better than to let himself care too deeply. Although it might already be too late.

He was coming to care for her as he'd cared for no other save Sina in years.

And there was his answer.

Silence had never taken change well.

And Vanya was changing everything for him.

He thought of her first, he thought of her last. He thought of her always.

He was started to thinking of her *for* always.

Down that road lay foolishness.

He knew he was best suited to life alone. It was a lesson he'd learned over and over again throughout his life.

But that was no reason for him to lash out, hurt her.

He needed to get this relationship where it belonged.

But still, he owed her a night. And while she didn't realize it yet, her rough night wasn't over.

Silence had dealt with the punch of a succubae attack, full on, enough to know how it was.

He knew how to evade it, how to shield better.

Since she hadn't been prepared, though, this wasn't going to be pleasant for her.

Through the walls, he could hear water running.

His body ached as he thought of her slipping off those sexy, skimpy clothes, slipping naked into the water.

Her body aching, needy...

Shoving away from the bar, he told himself, *One night.*

Then they would focus on her training. Only that. He would figure out how to put distance between them, without hurting her more than he already had.

He slid into the bathroom, seeking her out with his eyes.

She stood in front of the mirror, staring at her reflection.

There were tears in her eyes, and the sight of it was a dagger to his chest.

Coming up behind her, he slid his arms around her waist. Brushing her hair aside, he pressed his lips to the scars along the left side of her face. Such minor, paltry things to him.

But he knew they bothered her, knew she hated them.

She tried to turn away but he ignored it, kissing each mark, each wound.

"You look lovely," he murmured to her. Even as he did so, he marveled that he *could.*

Marveled that he could so easily speak to another.

Something he'd never thought he'd have again. God, how he cherished it...how he cherished *her*.

Was it any wonder he already felt so much for her? Although it went so much deeper than his ability to be able to speak with her. So much deeper. There were psychics among the Grimm, but never had he found one who could hear his thoughts. He was a psychic null, Will had told him. Some of them could skim his memories and lift random pieces there, but to hear his thoughts? For him to be able to *speak* again? It had never happened.

He could *make* himself heard with Vanya and it was a miracle.

She was the real miracle, though. And for a while still, she was *his* miracle. His miracle...and she was staring at him with a derisive smile on her face as she tried to push him away.

"I'm not lovely," she said, shaking her head.

"*I disagree.*" Resting his hands on her shoulders, he kissed her temple and then stared at the mirror, at their reflections. "*Lovely...so pale, so soft...*"

"Scarred," she added, turning her head so that the harsh light fell on them. "Let's not forget the scars."

"*How can I...they mark you as a survivor.*" He trailed his finger down one. There was more to those scars than just their appearance, he suspected. And looking into her eyes now, seeing the sadness there, he knew he was right. Only one person could have put that grief in her eyes. "*Your sister did this, didn't she?*"

She tensed against him. Her lashes lowered, shielding her eyes. "Yes. It wasn't her anymore, but yes."

"*There is nothing ugly in your scars,*" he said. "*You survived—you resisted what she could not. And don't tell me they weren't trying to take you as well. I know their kind too* well. You would have been young, scared...you should have been an easy mark."

Vanya turned her head, once more met his gaze in the mirror. A shaky sigh escaped her and she nodded. "They tried. I pushed them out. But I couldn't save her."

"By then, it was too late. You know that now. They are marks of honor...courage. Perhaps you see them as something ugly, but they are not." He kissed each one and then dipped his head, kissed her shoulder. "You are lovely, Vanya, so lovely. Know that."

When he touched her, she felt lovely.

She felt wanted...even if she was just his student, just a responsibility he'd been stuck with. At least he wanted her. For now. It was better than nothing, wasn't it?

Her head fell back against him as he reached between them, loosened the laces of her corset.

As it sagged then fell away, she took a deep breath, groaned. The thing was nowhere as tight as traditionally made corsets, she suspected, but still. That contraption took some getting used to. Silence's hands came up, cupped her breasts.

"I think damn near every man who saw you tonight wanted you." His voice was rougher, harsher as he used one leg to nudge hers apart. "I hated it."

The thought sent a thrill through her.

Or maybe it was the way he nudged her closer to the counter, bending her over... Big hands smoothed her skirt up, what little there was. Cool air kissed the bared flesh of her butt. Only the thong covered her and already she was wet, aching. One hand came up, stroked her. Vanya shivered.

"*You're wet.*" Harsher, rougher...all but growling through her mind, and she felt the backlash of his satisfaction shuddering through her. Her knees threatened to give out and she had to lock them simply to stand upright. He tugged on the thong and she whimpered as it rubbed against her, against the slick wetness of her sex, pressing between the cleft of her rump.

She heard a deep, harsh sigh escape him and she looked up, stared at his face, but he was staring down at her, long blond hair shielding him.

He gripped her hips and pressed against her, and she moaned at the contact, hating the clothes he still wore. Squirming against his hold, she tried to turn—she wanted him naked.

But he caught her hands, pressed them back to the counter. *"Be still..."*

"I can't," she snarled. Abruptly, hunger threatened to tear her alive. Lust was a ravenous beast in her belly and she wanted—*needed*—this. Shoving back against him, she glared at him in the mirror. "Damn it, I *can't*. I need..."

He shoved himself against her. Harder this time. As he did it, he slid a hand around to her front, unerringly seeking out the tight, rigid bud of her clit. *"This?"* he asked. *"Do you need this?"*

She whimpered. "More."

He pushed two fingers inside her, scissored them.

Closing her eyes, she rocked against him, riding his hand. But it wasn't enough—not enough. She reached back, clawed at him, found her hand fisted in the flowing leather of his jacket. "More," she begged.

Silence pulled away...left her alone.

She could have cried, but when she looked up, she saw that all he was doing was stripping out of his coat, his shirt. Barely aware of what she was doing, only that the hunger was still burning inside her, riding her, she stroked a hand down her middle, sank a finger inside her aching sex. The muscles clenched down tight and she groaned. It wasn't enough—

Damn it, where was this coming from...

A hand stroked her hair back from her temple.

"It's from earlier," Silence murmured, bending over her. *"I can help. If you want me to..."*

Turning her head, she stared into eyes of the palest blue. "Do it. Damn it, I can't stay like this..."

He stroked a hand down her arm, tugged her wrist back up and slid her fingers into his mouth. She gasped then whimpered, rocking back against him. He hadn't taken his pants off, though, and she couldn't wait—didn't want to. He guided her wrists back to the counter, still holding her gaze pinned with his. She stared, helpless, as he reached back.

She heard the rasp of his zipper and closed her eyes, sucked in a desperate breath.

"Look at me..."

"I can't...damn it, Silence, please." She groaned and pushed back. Ready to beg, all but dying.

"Shhhh..."

She felt him then. The hard, hot length nudging against her.

"Yes..."

"Do you trust me, Vanya?"

She stiffened, stilled—

Her eyes flew open and she stared at him. *Trust...* Looking at him, she tried to figure out what he was getting at. He curled a hand over her hip. *"Do you trust me?"* he repeated.

"Yes."

A pleased smile curled his lips. Then, before she could so much as draw a breath, he caught her hips, lifted her so that her feet left the floor. He buried himself, full length inside her.

She came in the next breath.

Impaled on his length, taken by the hard, fast surprise of it, she shuddered and shook with it, helpless.

Silence fisted a hand in her hair. The other hand came to her shoulders, pulling her back against him. Twisting against the deep, complete invasion, she cried out.

"Lean back against me," he ordered, slipping his hands down to her waist, *"and watch us."*

Stunned, she stared in the mirror.

Oh.

Oh, damn.

She still wore her skirt and her pendant. That was it.

Silence wore leather pants. And *her*. Her hair disheveled, mouth red, eyes bright and hot. She looked...wanton. Hot. And sexy. The scars, what she normally saw when she looked at her reflection, she hardly even saw them.

As she stared at their reflections, he lifted her up then down. She could see the swollen, reddened flesh of his cock, slick from her, as he penetrated her.

"Look at you," he growled, mind to mind. *"Look at how lovely you are. Touch yourself, Vanya. Stroke yourself."*

Vanya shuddered, her hands gripping his wrists.

"Do it."

Swearing, she reached up with one arm, clinging to him for balance. The other hand, she slid down. His gaze was locked on her hand, and the pale blue of his gaze glowed like fire. The tips of her fingers bumped against her clit. She hissed and arched. From Silence, she felt...something. It wasn't thought, wasn't emotion...

No.

It was a storm.

His head dipped and he raked his teeth over her shoulder. *"Touch...let me see,"* he demanded.

Helpless to resist, she began to circle her fingers around her clit. Slow at first, in rhythm to his deep, thorough strokes.

Then faster.

She shifted as much as she could, used her legs to awkwardly grip his and work back against him, clenching down tightly around him, shuddering at the pleasure of it. He stretched her, so hard, so thick, he almost bruised her.

Orgasm lurked just out of reach and she chased it, but she couldn't quite get there.

"Damn it, Silence," she snarled, shoving awkwardly back against him.

Over her shoulder, she saw him staring at her, a savage, harsh look on his face.

"You need more."

"I need to come."

"You need more. The succubae, incubae. It's like a fever. You need more."

"Then fix it." She didn't even care *how*—she just needed him to do something about this aching burn in her belly, this hunger that threatened to drive her mad.

"Fix it." His teeth flashed in a harsh smile. *"You're certain."*

"Yes..." She twisted her hips against his erection and sobbed out—it felt so damn good, but the ache only spread. Even the light touch of her fingers against her clit was more pain than pleasure right now. "I don't care how."

I don't care how—

Those words, even as they made some predatory, hungry monster inside him burn with hunger, were enough to make him pause. *"You should be careful with your words, Vanya,"* he murmured inside her mind.

Then, although the last thing he wanted was to pull away from her, that was what he did, separating their bodies.

She cried out, clinging to him.

Once he set her on her feet, she whirled around and reached for him, just as he was reaching for her. Hauling her against him, he stared down into her face, lifting one hand to touch her cheek.

"A succubae is a psychic thing...she sinks her power inside you, with each touch. It infects you—until you become immune to it. It will fade, but until it does, you will hunger, and you will burn. I can make it pass—if that is what you want?"

Vanya glared at him. "Didn't I already *tell* you that?" She curled her hands into the waistband of his pants, tugging him closer.

"You did...but didn't you notice how desperately you needed to come, and how it lingered just out of reach? You need more—it's a darker hunger, and you need something darker." Stroking her hair back from her face, he asked, *"Do you have dark hungers, Vanya?"*

She swallowed.

Staring at her, he backed away just enough, letting some air come between them as he fisted his hands in her snug skirt. *"Are you going to tell me?"*

Then he tore the skirt, shredding it in his hands.

Her eyes widened, and he saw the excitement flare before she covered it with a scowl. "Damn it, what are you doing?"

He hooked his hand in the front of her panties, a black silk thong he'd bought. He did the same thing he'd done with her skirt. And watched as the same excitement darkened her eyes.

Her hands flexed wide then curled into fists. Her mouth parted as her breathing sped up. Purely instinctive because neither of them needed to breathe so much anymore. He advanced on her, crowded her up until she came against the bathroom counter and still he moved in on her until their bodies were pressed snug against each other, her naked one pressed to his partially-clothed one. Still staring into her eyes, he caught her wrists, held them in his, watched her face as he started to rock against her.

Her head fell, the tumbled brown silk of her curls shielding her face from him.

"Look at me," he ordered.

She jerked her head up, stared at him, eyes dark and wild and wide. He tightened his hold on her wrists and she jerked against his hands.

When he didn't let go, an array of emotions ran through her eyes—everything from fear to hunger to nerves to excitement, even the edge of shame and guilt. Dipping his head, he raked his teeth over her neck. *"What do you hunger for, Vanya? Can you tell me?"*

"Silence..." Her body burned, blistered hot against his. "Damn it, would you just take me, please? I'm dying..."

"Take you how?"

She stilled. Once more she jerked against the hold he had on her wrists. Her breathing hitched in her throat, raspy, shallow. He pushed his thigh between hers. She was hot, hungry...so wet he could smell it and it was killing him.

He heard her swallow and then she looked up at him, her cheeks flushed hot—embarrassment, excitement...both... "However you want. However *you* want..."

"What about what you *want?"* He cupped her cheek, stared down at her. *"What you saw earlier—is* that *what you what? Do you want me to give you that?"*

Vanya shuddered. Then she licked her lips and whispered, "Yes."

"How much like that do you want it? How far do I go?"

She dropped her head against his chest, her hands gripping his waist, kneading his flesh restlessly. "I...hell. I want it as hard, as fast, as rough as you want to give it to me. As far as you want to go. Just...I don't think I'd want actual pain. I mean *real* pain. A little, I don't mind, but..."

Silence cupped her face in his hands, pressing his lips to hers. *"As if I could ever truly harm you."*

As those words echoed through her mind, Vanya's breath hitched. She sighed into his mouth then pulled back.

He rubbed his thumb over her mouth, so gentle. *"You are certain."*

She swallowed then nodded. "What we saw earlier, at the club...I...ah, I want that."

Silence stilled. It was a complete stillness, one that fell over him so completely, he could have been carved from marble. Only the glitter of his eyes showed that he lived.

Then, slowly, he trailed a hand up her side, cupped her cheek. *"You want it. Truly."*

"Yes."

Still moving with inexorable slowness, he pushed his hand into her hair, twining the short curls around his fingers. *"I will not harm you, Vanya. I swear it."*

Vanya smiled nervously. "I know."

He smiled, feathered a fingertip across one brow. *"If I do something that is too much, I want you to say chocolate. I will stop."*

"Chocolate?" She blinked, confused.

"Chocolate...the first time I saw your eyes, I thought of dark, melted chocolate."

"Oh, that's—"

Her breath caught in her lungs as he whirled her around and forced her flat over the counter.

Her heart skipped a beat. The icy-cold marble pressed her breasts flat. His hands, brutal and hard, gripped her hips, jerked her back against him. She felt him pump against her ass, felt his leather-clad thighs against hers. Thrown off balance, she went to push up on to her elbows, but before she could, he caught her arms, pinned her wrists at the base of her spine. *"Be still,"* he ordered.

She shuddered.

She felt the brush of his cock against her ass. Instinctively, she went to widen her thighs, but Silence caught her legs and held them penned together with his own. *"I said be still,"* he repeated again. Then he rested a hand on the curve of her ass, stroking lightly. *"You didn't listen—"*

Vanya opened her mouth. "I'm sor—"

He spanked her.

She caught her breath, shocked.

When he did it a second time, she cried out and jerked against his hands. Twisting her head around, she stared at him, shuddering, shaking—oh, fuck, he'd spanked her—

Their gazes locked. He rested his palm on the curve of her ass—waited. Just waited.

And she knew why.

To see if she'd say it, to see if she'd make him stop.

Hell no.

Deliberately, she jerked against his hands. "Damn it." Then, in case that wasn't enough, she once more tried to spread her thighs.

He spanked her again, staring into her eyes. She moaned and let her head fall back against the cool marble counter. The hot, burning sensation spread through her body—made every last nerve ending so sensitive, putting her body on red alert.

She could feel the throbbing length of his cock nestled against her butt, and she was tempted to rub against him, but she worried if she did, he might withhold that from her, and she wasn't about to risk that—she was so hot, so burningly ready.

"Maybe now you'll be still for me," he said after one final, hard spank.

Not likely, she thought. But she'd wait until he was inside her...

She felt the head of his cock probing against her entrance. With her thighs pressed together, it wasn't as easy, but she didn't dare try to spread them, anything to ease his entrance. And as he started to push inside, she whimpered, her breath catching—oh, that felt...amazing.

He let go of her wrists, and automatically she went to push up on to her elbows, but she didn't have the chance. Two seconds later, he had one wrist in each hand, pinning them on either side of her head. She lifted her head, met his gaze in the mirror.

His hands loosened a bit and she jerked against his hold.

He smiled at her. *"Do you want to fight me?"*

She whimpered. Blood rushed to her face. Oh, shit. This was...hell. She hadn't ever imagined acting out a fantasy like this, not for real.

Licking her lips, she gave him a jerky nod. Then she moaned as he pulled away.

"Turn around then."

She turned, faced him.

"Remember how to bring this to a stop," he reminded her.

"Yes," she whispered.

He still wore the leather pants, opened to expose his cock, thick and hard, wet from her. He looked...hot—so hot. And he stared at her with that remote, unreadable expression—the look of Silence.

It didn't change as he reached out, caught her wrists.

She jerked back.

It didn't stop him.

She struggled harder, panting a little. She went to kick him and he shifted, stepped—two seconds later she was on the floor with him on top of her.

An image flashed through her mind—from the club, the man stretched out over the woman, having his way with her seemingly resistant body. Vanya's instinct was to kick at him, but instead, she kept her legs clenched together, using only her hands and arms to shove at him, push, shove and even punch before he caught her wrists, penned them overhead.

Against her pussy, she felt the heated length of his cock, throbbing and hard.

"*Spread your legs,*" he told her.

"No."

"*Do it.*"

She sneered at him. "Make me."

He forced a knee between them, wedged himself in the cradle of her hips and shoved inside—it was hard and brutal, and she screamed at the abrupt, dark pleasure. His head came down, his mouth crushing against hers as he swallowed her scream.

She took a few seconds to enjoy the kiss and then she jerked her head away, as though she couldn't stand his kiss.

"*You opened your legs for me...I'll make you take my kisses too.*"

Looking back at him, she deliberately brought her thighs as close together as she could, clenching them tight, resisting his rough, deep penetration. It was enough to bring a cry to her lips, but she kept it behind her teeth.

"*That feels just as good, you know,*" he told her, rolling his hips against her.

Actually, it felt better—amazing. Her clit throbbed, burned. For a second, she forgot the game and just wanted to touch herself. She jerked against his hands and then stilled as he tightened his hold in response.

"Let my hands go," she snarled.

"*No.*"

"Damn it, Silence."

He dipped his head and bit her lip. "*Why?*"

She swore, struggled harder, arched up to grind her hips against him, seeking some contact, *any* contact that might ease the ache in her clit.

She saw the flare of understanding in his eyes. He shifted, his weight pressing harder on the hands he held pinned over her head as he reached between them with his free hand and started to stroke her clit. *"I'm going to make you come. Whether you want to or not,"* he told her.

"No," Vanya choked out. Even as her mind screamed, *Yes.*

"You'll come. Hard and fast."

Hard and fast—that's how he rode her, that's how he touched her, and still her climax eluded her.

All but sobbing in frustration, she gave a mighty jerk against his hold, managed to free her hands. Raking her nails down his arms, she twisted her hips against his, almost blind, all but deaf—

She needed to come, hurt with the need...

Silence rose, with her still impaled on his cock.

She moaned and arched, rubbing herself against him as he carried her out of the bathroom.

In the bedroom, he pulled away and bent her over the bed. It was a higher bed, the kind that left her feet dangling about two inches above the floor. She started to push up, but he put his hand on her neck, held her still as he shoved back inside her.

With one hand holding her head to the bed, and the other hand on her hips, she lay there, bent over and exposed for his pleasure—unable to find her own...it seemed.

Then he reached around and pinched her clit. Squeezed.

Vanya's eyes flew wide and she shoved upward, backward against him.

"*Be still,*" he snarled, his voice a harsh growl in her mind. It was erotic, sexy as hell...

"Damn it, Silence—"

He pushed her back down. "*Be still.*" He squeezed the back of her neck in warning.

She groaned and squeezed him with her inner muscles. Then she focused on the hand between her thighs, the one teasing and tormenting her clit. That...oh—

His thumb pressed against her ass.

Vanya stiffened.

Slick and wet, he pushed against her, slow and determined.

Panic fluttered, swelled.

She pushed upward again. "Silence, don't..."

"*Come for me, Vanya,*" he said, pinching her clit with one hand, forcing the thumb of his other hand deeper inside. And his cock, he rode her deep, hard, burying himself inside her with each stroke.

She jerked against his hold, thrashed around him.

"Close your legs again," he ordered. "*I like it that way—you're so tight and snug...especially when you're fighting it.*"

Vanya whimpered, already forgetting why she'd been struggling. Bringing her legs close together, she locked them at the ankles.

"*Good girl.*"

He pulled his thumb out, pushed it back it. As the same time, he gave her clit another hard, tight squeeze.

Oh—

Silence, holding on to his control by the skin of his teeth, watched as Vanya finally broke through whatever strange compulsion the sex demons had tainted her with.

She shattered and came, writhing around his cock, squeezing and milking him with exquisite sweetness.

With a snarl, he crouched over, bracing his hands by either shoulder as he began to pound into her. Her hot, slick walls clutched and squeezed and contracted around him, drawing the agony out.

It was the sweetest torture.

It was the most painful form of bliss.

And when it ended, all he could manage was to sink against her with his head resting on her shoulder as their bodies shook and sweat cooled on their skin.

They didn't *need* sleep...usually.

But they could sleep, and he was drifting close when he heard her whisper something.

"I think I'm falling in love with you, Silence..."

Chapter Seven

Then...

This was it, then.

Dying.

He lay in a fouled mess of blood, bile, piss and other foulness he did not want to think of, choking on his own blood.

His entire body hurt. He knew he had never hurt like this. Had not thought it was possible to hurt this way.

At least he was alone, though.

Alone.

It was better for him to be alone. It was safe this way.

Any time he had ever had another in his life it had led to pain—either imminent or eventual pain.

Best, he thought, to be alone.

Forever.

If only he had learned that lesson earlier.

Cold, now. So cold.

As the darkness loomed in closer, as the pain faded, replaced by a strange, gray numbness, he found himself wondering about the man, Will.

He had not seen him in months, not since that night he had spoken of promises and choices and strange men and secrets.

Had he been mad?

Or had he truly known this was coming?

Dare he make that choice?

Yes...

The cold faded. Warmth came. The pain was gone.

And then there was Will.

"It will be done soon, my friend. I promise. And I'll be here with you. You will not be alone."

He closed his eyes. No, he did not want to hear that last part.

Better to be alone.

Now...

Fatal error.

The second the words left her mouth, she'd known it was a problem.

Silence hadn't responded—it was as though he hadn't heard her.

But she knew he had.

It was there between them the next morning.

"So maybe if you're going to tell a guy you love him, you shouldn't blurt it out after a bout of rough sex, huh? Or maybe you shouldn't blurt it out after sex, period."

Vanya figured there might have been a better way to broach the subject, but she was tired of it lingering there between them. She wanted it dealt with.

Silence, though, he didn't seem to want to deal with anything. He looked up from the axe he was polishing, let their gazes meet for just a minute. Then he focused on the blade again.

"There is nothing that happened between us last night that you need to worry about."

"How about the fact that I said I think I'm falling in love with you? And the fact that it's wigging you out?"

"I'm not wigging out," he replied. *"And you are not falling in love with me. You're young and—"*

Vanya narrowed her eyes. "Don't," she said quietly, shoving back from the table.

He shifted his gaze back to her. *"Don't what?"*

"Don't tell me what I feel," she said. "I'm old enough to decide I can die so I become one of you, and I'm old enough to decide I can have kinky rape-fantasy sex, and I'm old enough to know if I'm falling in love or not."

Irritated and humiliated, she stood and turned away.

He didn't have to return her feelings. Damn it, she hadn't expected him to. But he sure as hell didn't have to be so damned patronizing, either.

"Vanya—"

In the doorway, she paused, looking at him over her shoulder.

Just looking at him made her heart clench. Just looking at him made her heart *hurt*, in a good way, though. It also made her body ache and hunger and throb. She'd hesitated before getting up this morning, and not because she'd blurted out something so embarrassing. But because she'd worried she'd feel self-conscious about what had happened. She hadn't, though.

She'd stood in the doorway, staring at him.

It wasn't until he'd looked at her that she became aware of uncomfortable silence caused by what she'd said...yeah, *that* made things awkward.

Staring into his eyes, she knew she hadn't been lying last night. If anything, she hadn't been clear enough. She wasn't *falling* in love with him. She was in love with him. She'd been falling in love with him bit by bit, day by day, and she'd known it *before* he'd brought to life hot, dirty dreams she hadn't even known she had.

"I know how I feel, Silence. If you don't like it, fine. You don't need to like it, and I'm not expecting you to feel the same way, but don't tell me I don't know what I feel," she said quietly.

"You're young. You're adjusting to a new life, and right now, I'm all you know—"

She narrowed her eyes. "Oh, bite me." Then she slammed her mental shields shut, blocking his mental voice out.

Damn him.

Slipping into the bedroom, she headed for the shower. She was still logy with exhaustion, but she'd be damned if she stayed around here right now. Later, when the tension wasn't knife thick, she'd come back. Later, after she'd cooled down, after her body stopped humming every time she looked at him.

Later...when he stopped looking at her like he feared she'd throw herself at his feet and cling until he produced a wedding ring.

Of course, there was a problem.

Standing in the middle of the bedroom, wrapped in a towel, she realized the only clothes she had were in tatters.

The short skirt had been decidedly trampish, but it *had* covered her. Now it wouldn't do that unless she held it in place. The thong wasn't in much better shape. The one piece of clothing that wasn't in tatters was her corset, but it wasn't like she could walk out of here wearing just that.

She didn't hear him, but the dance of cooler air along her flesh, along with the intensity of his gaze told her she wasn't alone.

Looking up, she saw him standing in the doorway.

Her lip curled when she saw he had his leather pants on from last night. He, at least, had clothes. And damn him for looking so good in them too.

His eyes, as always, were blank.

Bastard.

Tossing the torn scraps of her skirt on the floor, she snapped, "I realize you bought the damn thing, *teacher*, as apparently you're expected to provide for me, with me being your student and all. And I realize I all but begged you to rip the damn thing off, but I don't have anything to wear. Except a corset."

If she thought being bitchy might get a reaction out of him, she'd been expecting too much.

Instead, he bent down and grabbed something just outside the door.

A bag. No...not *a* bag. Her bag—one of them at least.

With her clothes.

Frowning, she closed the distance between them and grabbed it, slinging it over her shoulder and storming back into the bathroom. When had he had time to get her things?

Not that it mattered. She'd just make sure she got everything before she headed back to her room.

Somehow, she anticipated he wasn't just going to roll over on that one, especially considering how he'd knocked the little run down place last night. It wasn't a hellhole—yeah, it was run down, but the owner did his best. It was clean, it was quiet and it suited her just fine. He didn't ask any questions and he stayed out of her way too.

She rooted past the skimpy tramp clothes she had—not quite as nice as the things Silence had bought for her—past the workout gear until her fingers brushed worn denim.

Normal clothes. It would feel nice to wear normal clothes. She found panties and a bra tucked into the small side pouch, a black T-shirt. There weren't any toiletries, but she'd already used the ones the hotel provided here. She was dressed in under three minutes.

When she opened the bathroom door, she wasn't surprised to see Silence still standing there. "Did you bring anything else of mine over?" she asked, looking at a point past his shoulder.

She saw his hand lift and shifted her gaze, watched as he signed, *Yes.*

"Where are they? I'm going back."

You can't.

She snorted. "Watch me."

Vanya, be reasonable. That room is barely adequate for one person, much less two. And our actions are too easily noticed by others there. We're better off here. The staff is discreet, we can come and go without being noticed.

"I've never had any problems." She slanted a look at him. "Of course, I'm not a six-foot, pretty-boy blond. Tell you what, *you* stay here. I'll go back there. We can work out where we'll meet. You'll be happier without me underfoot, anyway."

Ignoring him, she tossed her bag on the bed. There weren't any shoes in there, so unless she wanted to go barefoot, she'd have to wear the boots he'd bought. That was fine. They were comfortable. She could walk it back to the hotel easily in those.

Although, maybe her tennis shoes were packed in the other bag—seemed like he was determined she wasn't going back—

She headed for the door but he beat her there, blocking it with one long arm.

She felt the press of his voice in her mind, but she resisted. Glaring at him, she said, "I don't want to talk to you right now."

It's a sad thing when we don't get what we want. But we're talking regardless. I don't consider you under*foot,* he said, his hands moving fast, sketching out the words with enough force that she realized he was feeling a bit of anger himself.

Oh, hey...he had emotions.

Lookie there.

"Well, I can't see how you wouldn't feel that way," she said, giving him a syrupy smile. "I'm young, foolish and I don't know jack about anything, and you're stuck with teaching me, and stupid me, I don't even know my own mind. Why *wouldn't* you consider me some annoying burden?"

When she went to duck under his arm, he caught her, his fingers gripping her tightly—not tight enough to hurt, but she wouldn't slip away unless she forced it. She was pissed off enough, humiliated enough to do just that.

But she'd already embarrassed the hell out of herself. Why make it worse?

Pasting a bored expression on her face, she lowered her gaze to his hand and then looked up at him. "Do you mind?"

He lifted his hand, cupped her face.

And once more she felt that press on her mind—harder this time, harder to ignore, harder to block out, and his voice was louder. Because he was touching her, she suspected.

Sighing, she looked away and lowered the shields.

Immediately, she felt the warmth of him as his thoughts rushed over her. She steeled herself against it, though, against him.

"You're not a burden. And I don't consider you a foolish girl. But that doesn't—"

Vanya slugged him, burying her fist into the hard wall of his belly as hard as she could. He doubled over, letting go of her arm. The sharp exhalation of air was worth the pain that jolted up her arm. "Don't keep telling me what I feel, Silence. I swear, you keep it up and I'll..." she paused, trying to figure out just what in the hell she could to do a guardian angel who'd been alive for a couple hundred years, at least, one who rarely showed any expression, one who didn't believe she knew her own mind. Shit, she knew next to nothing about him, in the long run.

Maybe...

No. Before that thought could even form, she pushed it aside. He wasn't right. She was. She knew she loved him. She knew what she needed to know, and it was ridiculously simple. She felt a connection to Silence that went deep, deeper than sex, deeper than some bond he might think existed because he was training her.

Hell. Will had shown up at the drop of a hat over the past few years to work with her, and he'd saved her neck more than once. But she hadn't ever once had a single romantic thought about him—the man freaked her out when he wasn't pissing her off.

Backing away from him, she stared at him. "If you keep telling me what I feel, I'm going take all of your axes and pour acid all over them."

His eyes narrowed.

"Isn't that rather childish?"

"Well, I *am* young," she said mockingly. "Us young people do foolish things."

Storming out of the room, she spotted her other bag on the floor. Along with the rest of her stuff. The weapons he'd bought for her, her own weapons, her meager stash of books. Scowling, she squatted by the bag and unzipped it. Her beat-up tennis shoes were on top. Hallelujah.

She stood up, turned and crashed right into him.

Swearing, she elbowed her way past him. "Leave me alone, damn it," she snapped. "I need some space."

This is foolish, he signed, some emotion finally starting to show on his face.

Frustrated.

He looked frustrated.

"Foolish." She glared at him as she sat down. Jamming her feet into her shoes, she tied them, disgusted to see that her hands were shaking. Hurt, humiliated, she swallowed and waited a few seconds before she said anything. She didn't want him to see just how hurt she was. She should have let it go. What did it matter if he believed her or not?

The knot in her throat was making hard it to speak, hard to think. She tried anyway and was surprised to hear that her voice was only a little shaky. "You think I'm being foolish—fine. Then let me be foolish. I need to get out of here and breathe, Silence. I need to clear my head, I need to think." Shifting her gaze to him, she glanced at him through her lashes. "I can't do it around you."

Without saying anything else, she grabbed her things.

If nothing else, she could be thankful that the weight of the bags was nothing to her now. Even the four-mile walk wasn't going to faze her.

She felt him pressing at her mind but ignored him.

I couldn't have screwed that up any more if I tried.

As the door closed behind her, Silence started to go after her.

Only to stop.

If it had just been temper on her face, he could have handled that. He often pissed people off. He didn't intend to, but he didn't go out of his way to avoid it, either. He could have ignored her anger.

But there had also been hurt. And wounded pride.

That he was having a harder time swallowing. He hadn't intended to hurt her.

She'd made him panic, but that wasn't her fault.

I think I'm falling in love with you...

He hadn't ever had a woman say those words to him.

It had terrified him.

Even as it elated him.

He hadn't let her see that, though.

Because he knew she was wrong.

She couldn't love him. She barely knew him. And soon, she would no longer need him—she would leave him.

She'd been thrust into a new world and he was all she knew. When things changed and she adjusted, it would be different. She would change, she would adjust…and then she would leave.

She wouldn't be one to fear change, not like him.

She wouldn't fear *not* being alone…he did. He needed to be alone because he had never known anything but grief when he truly let somebody else in. He hadn't done so since his mortal life—he hadn't even allowed Sina to get truly close, and she was his dearest friend.

No. He couldn't, wouldn't believe her. Although he was tempted…

Tension spiked in the air. Silence closed his eyes.

Not now, he thought.

Looking up, he watched as brilliant white flashed and Will emerged. It faded, leaving the two men staring at each other.

Wearily, Silence signed, *Go away.*

"Why? So you can stand here and feel sorry for yourself while your chance at happiness walks farther and farther away from you?"

Silence dropped into a chair, staring at Will. *She is not my chance at happiness. She is a new Grimm who was placed in my care, and I took advantage of her. She doesn't know how to adjust to this new world, and I should have taken better care of her than that.*

Will's bark of laughter rang through the room. "That's rich. Silence, you *have* met the same Vanya I know, haven't you? Mouthy, full of attitude, cocky little bitch?"

Silence narrowed his eyes. *Don't speak of her that way.*

"Why? It's God's honest truth. She *is* mouthy, full of attitude, rather cocky and she'll tell you herself that she is a bitch. And you think you took advantage of *her*?" Will shook his head. "My friend, it's just as likely she took advantage of *you*."

Silence looked away.

"She knows what she wants. She's not some naïve, foolish little girl. In truth, she never has been and whatever innocence she had died when her sister was taken by the succubae. She was still a teenager when I gave her the choice, and if I had allowed it, she would have been done with it then—it wasn't her time yet. It wasn't *your* time yet. You belong with her. Don't throw away this chance at happiness," Will said quietly.

Shaking his head, Silence signed, *She deserves somebody who can share with her, who can tell her all the wonderful things she deserves to hear. She deserves somebody who makes her complete. That man isn't me. I'm not complete by myself, how can I possibly be the man she needs?*

"That is the biggest load of bullshit I've heard in quite awhile," Will said.

Silence looked away.

"You're incomplete—because you cannot *speak*? Is that what you're saying?" Will shook his head. "It had better *not* be that—the boy in that tower knew better, had more strength of will, more courage than that. Have you changed so much since then that you'd see yourself as lesser because you can't talk the way I do? You *do* speak, you just do it in a different manner, and you know that."

Sighing, Silence shoved to his feet and paced. Even after all this time, Will could manage to make him feel the fool, the child. Shaking his head, he looked back at the other man. *That is some of it—I won't lie. But it's more than that. I—*

He stopped, hesitating. He was stripping himself bare here, leaving himself open and exposed. *I'm not complete. In here.* He tapped his chest. There was a void in there, something incomplete, something wrong—he'd always suspected it—it was what kept others from forming a bond with him, why he hadn't been able to bond with others. His mother had seen it, surely. It hadn't just been his gifts that had made her scream in terror, had it?

In his mind, he swore. *Mommy issues—damn it all.*

He shoved it aside and looked at Will. He wasn't going to try to analyze everything in his head right now. He knew what he needed to know—he wasn't what Vanya needed. He signed, *I'm not what she needs—I'm not complete, Will. She deserves better.*

"You weren't complete...until her." Will came over and sat on the coffee table, staring at Silence. Leaning forward, he braced his elbows on his knees. "As to being what she needs, I'd think that should be her call."

Silence scowled, shifting uncomfortably as a memory danced through his mind. He'd called her beautiful...and she'd argued.

Don't you think I should be the one who decides? he'd asked her.

As though he could follow Silence's thoughts, Will smiled. "It should be up to her," Will murmured.

Silence shook his head. *No. She deserves so much more. Damn it, I want her to have somebody who can make her laugh, somebody who can make her smile. Her life has been hell and this life will not be any easier. She should have somebody at her side who can tell her all the wonderful things she deserves to hear.*

Smirking, Will cocked a brow. "Oh, you're really reaching now...tell me something, Silence...can *you* talk to her?"

As Silence narrowed his eyes, the other man smiled.

"Can't you tell her all the wonderful things she deserves to hear?" Will asked gently. "Do you really think she *cares* if you say them out loud or she only hears them in her mind? I can tell you...she doesn't. It means something, you know...after more than three hundred years, you find somebody who *hears* you. You're a psychic null, Silence, and you know it. I can't hear a damn thing from you—and neither can our other psychics. If she can, it's because she's *meant* to. That means something."

He stood, moving to stand by the window, staring outside. "I can't make you do anything, though. This is your choice, and if you won't do the right thing, well..." Will shrugged. "If you insist on not following your heart, I can't force you to do otherwise."

He shifted his gaze, silvery eyes glowing. "But I can tell you this—you were right. Vanya's had a hard life. Too hard. And I won't torture her by keeping her with a man who refuses to love her. She deserves better and she won't find it if you insist on sticking to this path."

It took a minute for him to understand what Will was telling him. Silence curled one hand into a loose fist. *You're telling me that you will take her away from me.*

"Well, that would imply she is *yours*," Will said slowly. "And it sounds to me as though you're determined to talk yourself out of any possibility of that."

Denial screamed through him.

No—

The calm, rational part of him whispered, *This is best. This is the easiest way. You will be alone, as you prefer to be, and she will be—*

Silence turned away. She'd be away from him.

Shaken, he rubbed the heel of his hand over his chest, stunned to realize just how much it hurt to think about that.

"Is that what I should do, Silence?"

He looked at Will. He wanted to scream out, *No!* Even opened his mouth, although the word would come out soundless. His hands, suddenly clumsy, lifted. Then he stopped. Confused, he stared at Will.

Finally, he signed out hesitantly, *I don't know.*

Something that might have been disappointment glinted in Will's eyes. "Well, perhaps you need to figure it out." Then his gaze clouded and started to glow, like the moon coming out from behind a bank of clouds. "You might not have much time to make that decision either, old friend. Something just shifted things around a bit."

Something?

"You need to make a decision now—Silence. Either you're ready to reach for happiness or you're not. If you are, she's heading back to the hotel. If you're not...well, you be anywhere but there and that will tell me what I need to know."

I don't care for ultimatums. Silence glared at him.

"This isn't about ultimatums. It's about choices—do you want to be happy? Or are you going to be miserable and alone? It's that simple." Will shook his head. "You decide. But I don't have time to sit here and chat with you anymore."

Damn it—

But Will was already turning away.

The circle of light formed and Will stepped through it.

Silence lunged but it closed before he was close enough.

Chapter Eight

Vanya gaped at the stooped, bent little figure of the hotel owner. "What do you mean I can't have my room back? I told you I'd cover the damage—I've always been good for it, right?"

"It's not that." He sighed and wiped his balding head with a handkerchief he tugged out of his hip pocket. "It was your...ah...friend. And he's already covered the damage. But when he came by to check you out this morning, he offered me...well, some money if I didn't let you check back in, Miss Vanya. And I need the money. My wife and I, we're looking to move, and as soon as we can. Besides, I gave my word. So...I'm sorry. But you can't stay here."

Silence, you bastard.

She could have slugged him.

Wanted to slug him—was even tempted to storm back to the hotel and do just that.

Except he was probably expecting her to show back up.

Jackass.

Hell.

She'd roughed it on her own before.

She could do it again. Hitching one of the bags up, she gave the hotel owner a sour smile and went to turn.

There was a man blocking the doorway.

A shiver raced down her spine as she met his eyes.

Nothing human there...

Her skin wasn't doing that odd, weird little itch and crawl it liked to do with the incubae-type demons, though. He wasn't possessed by one of them. She didn't know what he was, either.

She'd only run across a few of the different kinds of things.

He barely glanced at her, a smile on his face. "Hello, Dad."

A weird sound—a rushing, pulsating sound—filled the air.

His heartbeat. The old man's heart. He was afraid. Shifting around so she could see him and the demonic, she eased her bag down on one of the broken-down chairs.

"Bobby. I didn't know you were back in town."

Bobby smiled. "Yeah."

Then he glanced at Vanya. "Maybe you can leave now. Me and my old man have some catching up to do."

She braced herself and lowered her shields. It was a good thing she'd had some practice because, otherwise, there was no way she could have hidden her horror at the intense, soul-sucking hunger she felt from him. Hunger from him...and terror from the old man.

Leave, Vanya. Leave while you can, the old man was thinking, even as he grieved for himself. His wife. *Damn you, Bobby...what happened to you...*

The rush of his thoughts was too much, unclear and erratic, so hard for her to follow. But she knew what she needed to know without his thoughts. The old man was human.

And the thing that had been his son? Wasn't. She was facing a demon.

Catching up...yeah. She could imagine the catching up they had to do.

She had enough of a read on Bobby to know what he planned on doing. He was going to feast on the old man over there. Then on his wife. Then on everybody else in their family.

Soul eater.

That's what this one was.

What had Silence called them?

Orin—

With a smile, she said, "Sure. I just need to check a few things first—I've got a long walk ahead of me." She pretended to root through the bag, palming the bladed staff Silence had ordered for her, using her body to hide it. As she straightened up, she pretended to sway, stagger.

She stumbled against the counter and the older man rushed around to catch her. As he steadied her, she caught his arm and did something she hadn't tried to do with anybody but Silence or her sister. *Get the hell out of here. Now.*

His eyes widened.

Out loud, she said plaintively, "I'm feeling a little dizzy. Can you get me a Coke or something?"

Get out of here. He wants to hurt you and I think you know it. Now get out.

His eyes slid past her to the man waiting just behind them.

Then they widened and he tried to shove her out of the way.

Vanya ducked just in time to avoid a blow that would have caved in the skull of a normal person. She shoved the old man backward and snarled at him. "Go!"

The old man shook his head and swallowed. "You don't know what you're doing. He's...he's dangerous."

"I know." She sighed and reached for her weapon. Turning, she faced the orin. Either the old man would run or he wouldn't. She couldn't do anything about him now.

The orin was her main problem.

He was eying her narrowly, an appraising look on his face. As she shrugged out of her denim jacket, a smile curled his lips. "You know, most of your kind wait until dark for this shit," she said, scowling.

"Well...what can I say? I was hungry."

She felt a strange press against her mind and smiled. "Sorry. You can't touch me. I'm sort of off-limits." She flicked her wrist and watched as the staff extended, blades emerging.

"Hmmm. But I bet you'd be tasty. Why *are* you off-limits?"

She twirled her staff and smiled at him—smiled, despite the fear quaking inside her. She didn't think she was ready to go solo against a bruiser. This one wasn't going to be distracted with a lure and false promise of sex, and there was something about the way he watched her that made her think he'd enjoy a fight.

"Why don't you figure it out?" she asked him, flashing him a cheeky smile.

She felt that nudge against her mind again, and this time, she was aware of something else as well—heat flaring against her skin, right where the pendant she wore rested between her breasts.

What did that mean? Silence had told her...Will.

Will's way of communicating with her, but what was he telling her?

She was going to take a stab in the dark and hope it meant he knew she was in trouble. She focused her thoughts on Will— she knew he could pick up on them, she just hoped she was strong enough to make herself heard. *I don't know what you're trying to tell me, angel-boy, but I'm in trouble.*

As she focused once more on the demon, she thought she heard a sigh, followed by a whisper of reply. *I know.*

The demon was still staring at her. Legs spread, hands pressed together, like he was praying, the tips of his index fingers pressed against his lips. "There's something curious about you," he murmured. "I can't quite figure it out...but I don't think I want the old man anymore. You'll be more fun."

Vanya smiled. "If only you knew."

She saw him tense, lunge—logically, she knew he was moving fast, should have been moving *too* fast.

But after months of working with Silence, she was prepared and she swayed to the side, evading him with ease. As she did, she struck out with her weapon, feeling the blade cut through muscle and flesh like butter. Blood flowed and he snarled.

"Oh, you'll pay for that, bitch..."

A prickle of unease rose along his spine as the tension from Will's departure faded. He recognized it too well.

Something new was moving through town—a new threat. He scowled, wishing he could ignore it. What he needed to be doing was figuring out what to do about Vanya—indeed, if he *should* do anything.

Alone is better...

And his heart raged at the idea.

Go after her. That was what his heart demanded. *Find her— duty will always be there, but will she?*

Will would take her away.

If he hesitated too long, Will would take her from him, and somehow, Silence understood she would be lost to him if he didn't take action *now*.

Yet he felt trapped—once more, imprisoned. But it was silence that held him captive, and it wasn't walls of stone, wasn't chains or even paltry rope.

It was fear.

His own fear.

So much time alone and he feared relinquishing that solitude.

So you will give up this chance?

He started to pace, shoving his hands through his hair, locking them behind his neck. Torn. Did he go after her? Did he let her *go*?

Swearing, he spun around and gripped a bedpost, staring outside. But he didn't see the vivid green of the trees, didn't see that brilliant blue of the sky, the quaintly done buildings.

He saw only her.

Will knew Silence's indecision—wished he could do something, say something. Impotence gnawed at him with greedy, small, sharp teeth. "Go," he whispered. "*Now.*"

Watching with his mind's eye, he smiled as Silence slowly lifted his head, his eyes narrowed, shoulders set. It was the look of resolution on his friend's face—

Duty be damned, Silence said, the words soundless. But Will knew what he said. Closing his eyes, he nodded. "Go on, then," he said softly.

He was about to close the link that let him watch when he saw something catch the other Grimm's attention.

Narrowing his focus, he saw what Silence had seen.

The television—

"We interrupt this program to bring you this live update."

Silence stared at the TV, barely aware of the female anchor's voice, barely aware of anything, save for the building in the background. He knew that building.

It was the club from last night.

"We have reports of gruesome murders that took place, right here in Ann Arbor. And even more upsetting—a hostage situation. The police who went in to investigate are being held captive—"

Silence swore.

And somewhere inside, he felt something break. His heart, he supposed.

He might have been able to ignore the bothersome call of duty, but human lives?

No.

The day he did that was the day he became a monster himself—he killed the monsters, he didn't become one.

Turning away from the television, he gathered his weapons, dressed.

Something hot, wet rolled down his face and he absently brushed it away.

In the end, he supposed, this was how it was meant to be.

Perhaps this was God's way of reminding him of that.

Silence was better alone.

"*Damn* it," Will bellowed.

Mandy flinched as the sound rang through the cabin.

Okay, she'd seen the man upset before, but outright furious.

Peering around the corner, she blinked at him. "Ahhh...are you okay?"

He shot her a narrow look. "Apologies. Were you resting?"

"No." She made a face at him. "I'm tired of resting. And I *don't* need to keep resting that much. I was actually *reading*, thank you. What's up? What did I do now?"

He frowned. "It wasn't you." Then he shook his head. "I must go."

Before she could say another word, he was gone, in that familiar flash of light.

Silence weighed his options.

He could risk being seen by going in now, saving the policemen inside the building, while forcing to Will deal with the fallout.

Or he could take some time to plan, figure out a better way inside that wouldn't involve him being seen, but it would probably mean some of the hostages would die.

None of them were ideal.

He was fifty yards away, watching from the relative anonymity of the crowd, a pair of black shades shielding his eyes as he studied the layout and ran through his decidedly short and limited list of options.

Around him, the crowd was wary, giving him strange looks, and while they weren't overly obvious with it, none of them wanted to stand too close to him. He was used to it. Mortals were never particularly comfortable around him. They hadn't been comfortable around him even in life.

He was acutely aware of the looks they gave him, acutely aware of the distance they worked to give him.

When he felt a familiar ripple in the air, he frowned. Moments later, Will emerged from the crowd, coming to stand next to him. Silence might have been a little thrown off by his appearance, if he'd care enough.

Will wasn't in his trademark white—like Silence, he wore dark, utilitarian clothes, his silvery hair pulled back into a tight club and tucked under his shirt.

"You don't need to be here," Will said shortly. "I'll handle this."

Silence shook his head. He'd allowed this—he should have been more careful.

"Don't you have something *else* you'd rather be doing?"

Silence sighed. Then he signed, automatically using the language they'd used before he learned ASL. *Yes. But this is where I belong—I made mistakes here and I won't let mortals suffer for them. And I suspect this is God's way of telling me I shouldn't be doing something else. After all, it was right when I was leaving to go after her...no coincidence, that.*

"Don't be a fool."

That's exactly why I'm here.

Will swore. Then he shook his head. "Let's get out of the crowd. I'll get us inside and we'll deal with this—maybe then you can think clearly again, and then you can go do what you need to be doing."

But as they made their way out of the crowd, an icy-cold sense of foreboding flooded Silence. He found himself thinking about Vanya. He wished he would have told her—even if it was only once—that she'd mattered to him. A lot. In ways no other ever had.

In less than five minutes, Will had found a place remote and quiet, and Silence waited as he formed his doorway. Just before they would have passed through, he caught Will's arm.

If I fall—will you do me a favor?

Will narrowed his eyes. "You're not going to fall. And if you have words for your woman, you'll give them to her yourself."

Silence shook his head. *Something dark and cold looms before me.*

"Perhaps it's the fate that awaits you if you push her away."

He stared at the other Grimm, waited.

"Silence..." Then he sighed. "Yes. If that's your wish. But if you fall, you know I can follow you, and I will. I'll follow you and make your resting days a nightmare. You'll have no peace—know that."

I've never known peace—why should I expect that to change?

Then he signed a simple message, thankful, for once, that he didn't need to rely on his voice. Because the knot in his throat wouldn't have allowed him to speak anyway.

Will nodded and then looked away. "But you're not going to fall, damn it. It's a nest of succubae. If we can't handle that, there's a problem."

She was bleeding, bruised and pretty sure that she'd broken something—or several somethings.

The good news was that the demon in front of her was in the same shape.

The bad news—and no, the injuries weren't the bad news—he was getting pissed.

The couch went airborne as he stalked her through the little house. Thankfully the hotel wasn't connected to the office, currently located in said trashed house, but it wouldn't be long before somebody heard them, she feared. Heard them. Reported them.

It wouldn't be the hotel owner and his wife, though.

She'd just glimpsed them busting ass out of there, speeding off in a truck like the hounds of hell were after them.

"You just lost your lunch," she said, smiling at him despite the way it made her busted lip hurt.

He snarled at her. "I'll make do with you."

"Haven't you figured it out?" She laughed at him. "You *can't*. I'm useless to you, as far as food goes."

"Then I'll just rip your guts out and fuck your corpse," he said grimly. "You'll be good for something."

She saw his muscles coiling and she braced herself, waited until he was sailing through the air before she shifted and brought her staff up. He still managed to twist away, right before he would have impaled himself on it too—damn it.

He laughed at her as she stumbled away. "You're good, you little bitch. But you're not good enough."

She suspected he was right.

Her hands were slipping on the weapon too, and this time, when he came for her, she didn't move in time. He managed to wrench it away, hurling it across the room. The blow to her stomach that followed had her doubled over. The one to the back of her head sent her sprawling to the floor.

He crouched over her and she cringed as he eyed the silver chain around her neck.

"Well, well, well...I had a feeling," he muttered. "But, baby, they should have trained you better. You're not good enough to be out on your own yet."

"What makes you think she's alone?"

Chapter Nine

They didn't dare use the shadows yet.

Not until they knew what the succubae were doing with the cops.

Although guessing by the breathy moans and hoarse grunts, it wasn't hard to figure out.

Up ahead, something lay on the middle of the floor.

Something slippery, wet...and broken. It had been a man, once, although it was hard to tell at first. Guilt tore at Silence and he closed his eyes. He should have taken more care last night.

Will touched his shoulder. When he looked at him, Will signed slowly, *You were worried for Vanya—your concerns were for her.*

Silence shook his head and didn't answer. It was no excuse.

He could have gotten her out of here and returned.

His carelessness had led to this.

As they drew closer to the sounds of sex, he drew his battle axe. *I'll deal with them if you'll handle the mortals, get them someplace where they can be rescued with the smallest chance of exposing us.*

Will gave a short nod and signed, *We need to distract them, draw them out. Any ideas?*

Silence smiled grimly and lifted his axe. Slowly, methodically, he started to thump the flat of it against the wall.

"Subtle," Will muttered, shaking his head.

As far as Silence was concerned, *subtle* could get fucked.

She didn't know that voice.

Rolling her head to the side, she glimpsed a face—nope. Didn't know the face either. But something about the man standing in the doorway made her breathe easier—or at least she would have, except for the agony of the broken ribs.

They were healing, knitting together—she could even *feel* that, but damn, it still hurt—she hurt more now than she had when she'd taken a beating as a human.

The demon turned and looked at the stranger.

"Oh. It's you. I thought I'd killed you."

The man gave him a boyish, charming smile. "Oh, I'm hard to kill...apparently even harder than you."

"Hmmm. What's it going to be this time, Grimm?" The demon cast a glance down at her.

Vanya shuddered, forced herself to her hands and knees. She didn't like the speculation in that thing's eyes. Not at all.

He bent to grab her and she gathered her strength, forced herself to roll away. It wasn't graceful and it wasn't pretty, but it put a few feet between them. Spitting the blood in her mouth onto the floor, she sneered at him. "Find another bargaining tool," she suggested.

The other man laughed—man...Grimm?

The pendant between her breasts heated.

"Oh, you're feisty. I like that," he said.

"How sweet of you." She panted, pressed a hand to her side. "Do you know this asshole?"

"Sadly, yeah. Been trailing after him for a few months. He's slippery." Then he smiled. "He's not getting away this time."

The demon grinned. "Don't so sure."

Then he blinked—looked stupidly down at his chest.

He was staring at the same thing Vanya was staring at—the large, bleeding hole there.

As he toppled to the ground, his face lifeless and slack, Vanya looked back at the Grimm and saw him tucking a gun into a holster that made her think of tumbleweeds, shootouts and saloons. "A gun? I can use a gun? That was too damn easy," she muttered, fully aware of the borderline whine creeping into her voice.

"That's why a lot of the older bastards don't like them. Me, I'm all for the 'line 'em up, shoot 'em down' premise. Of course, the first time I caught this one he was in a crowd—can't go shooting people down in public anymore." The man frowned, tugged at his lower lip. "People freak out about that."

Vanya gave him a weak smile. "Imagine that..." She grunted and struggled to her feet, swaying a little. More blood gushed from the ragged wound in her side.

Her unexpected rescuer scowled. "He really did a number on you. How new are you, anyway?"

"Changed over a few months ago." Her mouth felt horribly dry. And her tongue felt thick. She squinted at him, but his face was wavering back and forth in front of her.

She stumbled, saw the floor speeding up to meet her. But then hands caught her. Steadied her. She gasped as pain flooded her entire body.

"Sorry."

"'S okay. Maybe…ah, I think maybe I should siddown or sumpin," she mumbled, looking up at him.

He had freckles, she noticed. Strange thing to notice.. He had freckles and coppery-colored eyes, coppery-colored hair that matched those coppery freckles. And he looked like he ought to be smiling, all the time. But he wasn't smiling now.

"You can't sit, lady. Damn. A few months. We have to get out of here. *Now*."

"Huh?"

She looked down, staring at the body on the floor. "But ish—*it's* dead."

"I'm getting your things. Then we'll get out of here. Damn it, this is a mess. Going to have to clean it up too…"

Her head started to spin.

The last thing she remembered was that she still needed to yell at Silence.

Finn caught her before she could collapse.

He had her blood all over him. She was healing too slow.

"Damn it, why are you alone right now?" he muttered.

She should have had somebody with her for another few years.

He didn't have time to worry about that right now, though. He wasn't even supposed to *be* here, really. Just chasing after the now-dead orin. Why there was a broken, abandoned baby

Grimm in his arms, that was a mystery he'd have to figure out later, after he'd cleaned up the mess.

Of course, his idea of cleaning up was messy.

She was tucked into his car across the street when the flames started. Finn remained close by, keeping the fire hot and bright until the central area was destroyed—all but the body of the demon. Enough remained of him for the family to identify and bury if they wanted, but he knew too much about this orin—he'd killed his kid sister a few months back, and the parents knew. They wouldn't want him. Once he was sure the fire had burned hot enough to destroy any other possible evidence, he used his power to dampen it then extinguish it.

As he strode back to his car, he felt a touch on his mind.

I hope you were careful.

"Hiya, Will!" he said cheerfully. Will hated the way he liked to burn things.

Were you?

"Hey, I'm always careful."

There was a sigh. *You've got a young Grimm with you, yes?*

As he opened the door to his car, he paused then shrugged. After more than a hundred years, you'd think he'd be used to how Will seemed to see all, know all. He wasn't. "Yeah, I got her. She's a mess too. You need to come get her, figure out what's going on. She shouldn't be on her own yet."

Right now, she's your responsibility. I'm...otherwise engaged.

Finn frowned.

"Hey, wait!"

But Will was already gone.

Silence whipped both axes up, crossed them over his head to block the downward stroke of a sword just before it would have split his head open.

A trap that wasn't a trap.

That's what this was.

The succubae had used their more *obvious* presence to hide others, something neither Silence nor Will had realized until it was too late.

Will had to get the humans out, though, and not just out of the building, but *away*. If there were both succubae and orin here, they were in a world of trouble. Succubae, incubae, they weren't thinkers—save for the king or queen. But put the king or queen together with even *one* of the orin and there were problems.

The soul-suckers were deadly, and there were two of them in here.

Well, one now. The other had one of Silence's throwing axes buried in his skull. The human body it inhabited couldn't survive *that*.

He swiped out with his smaller axe, barely missed the orin's throat. The orin backed away, twirling his sword with the ease of one who knew how to use it. Silence felt the power in that thing, the age. He'd been around awhile. Sucking up too much power, too many souls, and he'd learned how to hide himself too, Silence suspected.

"I saw you here last night with your little whore," the orin said, panting. "Tell me something, Grimm. How come you all get to do all that fornicating, but it's frowned upon when *we* do it?"

Silence brandished his axe—saw the demon's gaze skip to it. That was when he moved forward, kicked the thing square in the chest. As he flew back, Silence advanced.

Two of the succubae flew at him, their nails curled into claws.

"It's a shame, you know. I bet she was a good little fuck," the orin said, smirking. "I'll be sure to ask."

Ask...

Silence narrowed his eyes, unsure what game the thing played.

"I had one of my boys go to that hotel. We've got the owner's son, you know. That's why he's so hungry for money. He wants out of town, away from here before my boy comes back looking for him. Which was...*today.*"

Lies, he told himself.

Just lies.

It must be, because if there was truth in those words...if there was an orin lying in wait at the hotel—

It was a distraction on the demon's part.

Silence knew it.

And it was the most effective one available. Because now he couldn't think anything but ending this and getting out—he had to check on Vanya. If he'd gone after *her* instead...

Will had to spend precious time undoing damage, restoring the minds of the mortals he'd been able to save.

There were two he couldn't help. They'd given in to the lure of the succubae and already their minds were polluted with the demon taint, too twisted now, and they weren't fighting it at all. The poison was too deeply embedded.

But those he could save, he was doing everything he could to remove the stain—

Not just healing their bodies but *undoing*.

What was done became undone.

It took longer, it drained him.

It was necessary, though—they shouldn't have those memories or those wounds.

He left them there, in a storage building behind the club. Their minds were blank after they'd entered the club. He didn't like that because he knew that often the *lack* of knowledge was as traumatic as knowing what had happened. But they couldn't know what they'd been subjected to—they'd seen enough to realize something *not* right was going on, and that had been before their attacks. Glowing eyes, abnormal strength—no, the Grimm definitely couldn't leave that knowledge in the hands of police. Too much depended on it.

Weariness plagued him as he built his doorway.

"Back into the trenches," he muttered, a grim smile on his mouth.

It faded a second later as the thick miasma of blood, gore and death all but choked him. Three succubae rushed him and he flung a hand at them. Light, pure and burning, tore through them—it left no mark as it killed them, sending the demons back to the netherplains and leaving empty human husks on the floor.

There were bodies everywhere. Too many. There hadn't been this many—

A hot, burning sensation pierced his mind.

Death—

He saw it unfolding in his, even saw himself—his back.

Spinning around, he saw Silence, watched as he swung with his axe.

Saw the succubae behind him. Saw her lift the sword even as the orin in front of Silence hefted his own blade.

It was a blood-curdling scream, one that would haunt Finn's nights. She'd been limp in the seat, bleeding all over the good leather while he drove and mentally bitched. Abruptly her eyes flew open and she started to scream—back arched, hands clawing at her chest, her entire body shaking.

Her eyes rolled back into her skull and she started to convulse—Finn recognized it, but he hadn't ever seen that sort of thing from *their* kind. A Grimm having a seizure?

Reaching up, he gripped his pendant. "Will? There's something really freaky happening with your baby Grimm here..."

He wasn't sure if he'd get an answer.

He did, and it was a loud, furious snarl. *I'm not surprised, but you'll have to deal with her on your own—her man's about ready to die and I can't help you if I'm supposed to save him too.*

"Her man?" Finn echoed blankly. Then, shaking his head, he pulled the car over. Didn't matter—none of it mattered.

She was still twitching, her body jerking when he put the car in park. But as he turned to her, she stiffened, one fisted hand pressed to her chest. A long, tortured moan escaped her lips. "Silence..."

"Silence?" Finn closed his eyes. Damn. Somebody had really decided to do a number on this girl if they'd paired her with *that* one.

Then, as he stared at her, tears began to seep out from under her closed eyes. Guilt struck him in the heart, hard and fast. He winced. So the guy was freakishly scary—had a way of staring at you that made a man feel like he could see right through you. So the guy barely seemed to be *of* this world—even for one of them. If this girl had fallen for him, well...that was what mattered. She obviously didn't lack for guts and she couldn't be a bad sort, right?

For that matter, neither could Silence.

Even if he was decidedly strange.

She was still crying silently in her sleep. Unable to ignore it, Finn awkwardly hugged her and stared out the window. He wanted to reach out to Will, ask him what he should tell her when she woke up.

But maybe it was best that he not know anything yet.

Chapter Ten

She woke to smell the sea.

Licking her lips, Vanya sat up and found herself the focus of a pair of dark brown eyes. A woman sat at the foot of the bed, her legs folded. She had a delicate, almost ethereal beauty. Her strawberry-blonde hair was pulled into a stubby ponytail, leaving the fine bones of her face unframed.

The woman cocked her head and asked, "How do you feel?"

Vanya blinked and just stared at her.

Her mind clamored with about ten bajillion questions—starting with *Where in the hell am I?* Second question was—*Where was Silence...?*

But she was afraid to think much more than that because, for some reason, just thinking of his name left her eyes stinging with tears and her heart aching something fierce. It wasn't just that argument, either—something had happened. Something bad. The nightmares that had chased her while she slept hinted at it, but she'd never fully *seen* anything.

Taking a deep, slow breath, she swallowed. Her throat was horribly dry. "Tired. Confused. Who are you?"

"I'm Perci." She smiled. "I can't blame you on the confused thing—you've had a rough start, I think."

"Rough start?" Vanya echoed.

Perci grinned and pulled on a silver chain, revealing the pendant that had lain tucked under her white tank top. "Relax. You're with friends."

Even though the woman seemed nice enough, Vanya didn't know her. Shaking her head, she said, "Wearing that isn't enough to make you my friend, Red."

"Ouch."

Now *that* voice at least sounded a little familiar. Looking over, she saw a man in the doorway. Yes, familiar—no name, though. He had a friendly, appealing face, with a smattering of freckles across his nose, coppery-golden eyes and coppery-golden hair. She could remember thinking he looked like he'd be the kind to smile a lot. And he was smiling now, although it was a tired one, strained.

"I know you," she said absently.

"Yeah. You kind of got between me and an orin I was after." His mouth twisted in a grimace. "He messed you up pretty bad—those things aren't easy for a baby Grimm to handle."

Vanya narrowed her eyes at him. "I wasn't exactly lying down and making it a piece of cake for him."

"No." He shook his head. "You did a number on him, that's a fact. But he worked you over too. You've been under almost a week while your body healed itself."

A week—

She blinked, shaking her head. "Did...did you say a week?"

"Yeah."

Okay...she licked her lips again, but her tongue was so dry, it didn't do any good. "Could I get some water?"

"Sure." Perci gave a smile and rose off the bed, all long limbs and easy grace. She paused at the door, gave the man a strange, enigmatic look and then disappeared.

"Ah...so a week."

"Yes." He had his arms folded over his chest, and he watched her with a strange, shuttered look.

"Has...um, has anybody come looking for me? I...well, my trainer, maybe?"

He shook his head. "I sent word about you once I figured out how young you were. I was told you're my responsibility for now."

That was a dagger strike, straight to the heart. "You...you were *told* that?"

He gave a short, terse nod.

Feeling the burn of tears, she looked away.

She heard the soft fall of footsteps. "Here's your water, Vanya."

She waved toward the table. "I'll drink it in a minute," she mumbled. When she was a little less likely to puke it up.

"Were you told why I was placed with you?" she finally asked.

He hesitated for so long, she finally turned her head to look at him. Perci must have left the room again. He had a pained look on his face as he slowly said, "I wasn't really told much of anything, Vanya. Just that I'd be the one dealing with you for a while."

"Dealing with me," she whispered. She blew out a breath and then nodded. "Okay, then. Since you're dealing with me, I guess I should know your name."

He gave her a faint smile. "Just call me Finn."

"Finn." She reached for the glass of water on the table. "If you don't mind, I'm still very tired."

"Of course."

Perci found Finn out by the bay.

"You look pissed," she noted. "I think I've seen you pissed off exactly three times in your life. I mean, *really* pissed."

"She thinks Silence sent her away," he growled. Stooping over, he picked up a rock and hurled it into water. It hit with enough force that the spray from its impact almost reach the shore. He slanted a look at her. "I felt like I'd punched her or something, seeing that look on her face."

"I take it you're not supposed to tell the truth—that Silence nearly died."

"Shit." He curled his lip. "Since when did I ever do what I was *supposed* to do?"

"Um...never?" She gave him a beatific smile.

When he looked back at her, she cocked a brow. "You've never listened to rules. Some of us do out of respect for Will. Some of us do because we were born in a time when we simply obeyed those in positions of authority. Others...like you...decide when you'll obey rules, and when you won't. If this is burning your ass so bad, why are you listening?"

"Because I hear her crying for him." He looked away. "And something in my gut tells me there's more to their story than what I know, which by the way is *nothing*. She's a mess of pain, and there's something seriously weird going on. Silence is a freaky bastard, but he wouldn't have let her just trample off to face an orin on her own."

"Easy answer there—he didn't know about the orin," Perci offered.

"Still." Finn shook his head. "I don't know what's going on. I'm not going to go throwing out information that might make things worse for her." Then he gave her a faint smile. "Of course, she's awake now...maybe I can get some information out of her."

But as the two of them started toward the house, the both grew aware of a new presence.

It wasn't one Finn recognized.

Perci, though, did.

As she stepped into her house, her husband Jack was sitting at a table with a woman she knew—but didn't care for.

Her name was Sina.

She was one of the older Grimm. Very old. Just looking into her eyes was unsettling. Something about her made Perci's skin crawl, and it wasn't just the fact that there was no love lost between them.

Jack shot Sina a narrow look. "I was out picking up some stuff at the store and this woman attached herself to my ass, wouldn't leave. She said she needed to speak with our guest and it would be better if she came in with an escort, versus just strolling up."

"Yeah." Perci gave Sina a tight smile. "If she'd just strolled up, I probably would have told her to get the hell out."

Sina sighed. "And to think I helped you reconcile with your true love."

"And no doubt, you did that out of the goodness of your heart."

Jack gave Perci a puzzled look, but she ignored it, still staring at the other Grimm.

"Why are you here, Sina?"

"To speak with the young one you're sheltering," Sina said, sipping from a glass of wine. "She doesn't belong here with you."

Finn smirked. "No? I was told she was my responsibility, and since I'm here, I figure she belongs where I am."

"She's not yours." Sina barely glanced at Finn. "She is needed elsewhere and she's taking too long to get there. I'll speak with her now."

As Sina rose from the table, Perci moved to block her. "You'll speak with her when I decide you can, Sina. You're in *our* house. She's *our* guest and she just woke up. You're not going to go in there, intimidate or terrify her."

"Do you really think you can stop me?" Sina cocked her head, studying Perci.

Perci bared her teeth in a mockery of a smile. "You don't go out in the real world much anymore, witch. I wonder if you even remember how to fight. I do it every day. Yeah. I can stop you."

Jack moved up to stand behind Perci, a strong, solid presence. His hand curved over the back of her neck. He pressed a kiss to her temple.

But to her surprise, he didn't volunteer his very solid ass-kicking skills.

"Maybe if you could explain why it's so important that you talk with her."

Perci turned and gaped at him.

He grimaced. "Sorry, princess. I just..." He scowled and shot Sina a dark look. "I remember bits and pieces of her. She wouldn't be here if it wasn't important. Although she doesn't need to be such a domineering bitch."

Sina started to laugh. "It would appear that no matter what life you live, Jacques, you will always state things exactly as you see them." With an amused smile on her lips, she looked back and forth between Jack and Perci and then she nodded. "Very well. I'll explain...briefly."

She turned around, her long skirts swirling around her ankles. She took her place back at the table, a queen seating herself before peasants, Perci thought.

Then she focused eerie, otherworldly eyes on them. "Silence is not long for this world. It's not his body that fades, but his soul. His heart." She angled her head. "That girl...she's already become his heart, but he fades for fear that she doesn't feel the same."

Off to the side, Finn swore.

Sina glanced at him. "Yes." Then she looked down, black hair falling to hide her face. When she looked back up, the aloof mask she wore had fallen away and she looked tired and sad. "I *cannot* tell her to go to him. If I do, it will change things, alter their course too heavily. But Silence is my dearest, oldest friend and nor can I sit by and wait for this silly chit to decide she needs him."

"That silly chit thinks Silence sent her away," Finn growled, shoving off the wall, glaring at Sina.

"Then she doesn't really know him all that well, does she?" Sina demanded.

"Oh, come off it." Finn snorted. "If Silence is fading away, as you put it, because he thinks she doesn't love him, then she's entitled to think he sent her away—it sounds like some massive lack of communication on both sides."

Sina opened her mouth. Then closed it.

Perci tilted her head back, laughing. "A lack of communication...from Silence. Imagine that. Sina, could it be that your good friend Silence hasn't *told* her he has feelings for her? Why shouldn't she think he sent her away?"

"Oh, do shut up, Percinette," Sina muttered. She sighed and rubbed her brow. Then she lowered her hands, folded them in her lap. "Silence is...well, yes, it's likely he wouldn't have told her of his feelings. I cannot blame him. This girl, she's so young, and his life has taught him that he is best suited to being alone." She paused, shaking her head. "I cannot blame him—life has treated him harshly, and it hasn't been much kinder since he crossed over."

Perci scowled, vaguely aware of an uncomfortable, itchy feeling shifting through her. Something that felt a lot like guilt. She'd known Silence for a long time—known him, avoided him as often as she could. He made her uncomfortable.

Aware that Sina was staring at her, she looked up.

"He makes many people uncomfortable," Sina said quietly. "He knows it—even enjoys it at times."

Rising from the table, she moved to stare down the hallway. "His time is fading. Will you help me or must I go through you?"

Perci sighed. Then slowly she stepped aside. "I'm not doing this for you," she said softly.

"Oh, trust me, Percinette," Sina's mouth twisted in a smile and her blue eyes glowed, "I know that very well."

Chapter Eleven

Silence drifted in darkness.

He knew he wasn't alone.

Will was there.

Will's presence was some vague comfort, but it was distant and cold.

The pain that had racked his body, so obscene and bright, had faded.

Everything faded.

Except thoughts of her.

Vanya.

Where was she?

The only thing he knew was that she wasn't with him.

And although he wasn't truly alone, although he knew he had a friend he trusted at his side, he felt more alone than he'd ever felt. He should have been at ease with that because hadn't he already decided it was better that way?

But as he drifted farther and farther into the darkness, all he wanted was to feel her at his side. He reached out to her, tried to whisper into her mind.

Where are you...? I'm sorry, Vanya. Will you come back?

But the words fell into the vast darkness around him, into the nothingness.

Where are you...come back...

The whisper was faint, so faint, tickling her mind, tugging her from a restless sleep.

Flinging an arm over her eyes, she tried to retreat back into sleep.

"He calls out for you and you would sleep through it?"

Vanya jerked upright in the bed, automatically reaching for a weapon. But there wasn't one.

Something told her it wouldn't do much good against the strange woman sitting at the foot of her borrowed bed.

Strange, strange woman...

Her eyes were blue, but not just one shade of blue. As Vanya willed her racing heart to slow down, the woman's eyes shifted from the blue of the skies outside the window to the deep blue of midnight to a shade almost as pale and icy as Silence's. It wasn't just the way they changed shades, though. Wasn't even the fact that her eyes seemed to glow a little either—although *that* was freaky.

There was a look in her eyes—something that barely seemed human. Too ancient, too wise, too...something.

She wasn't particularly beautiful—her features were too unique for that. Her skin was a dusky shade of gold, startling against her blue eyes. Her hair was darker than pitch, falling ruler-straight down to the small of her back. Her mouth, ripe, full and lushly red, curved in a faint smile as Vanya stared at her.

Their gazes locked, and Vanya felt her heartbeat stutter. She all but tore her eyes away—this woman wasn't human.

"No more human than you," she murmured.

Hissing out a breath, Vanya shot her another look, although she didn't dare let their gazes connect again. Shaking, she clambered out of the bed, looking around for something to wear. "I don't care to have strangers digging through my mind," she snapped.

"I'm not digging." The woman shrugged. "I cannot help that sometimes thoughts are there for me to see. Any more than you can help that sometimes thoughts are there for you to hear."

"Yeah, but that doesn't mean I have to *listen*—or that you have to *look*," Vanya snapped.

"But I like to look." She smirked. She drew a knee to her chest, resting a chin on it. "He calls you. Are you going to hide away like a child?"

Silence—

Vanya swallowed, shivered as the ghost of his voice drifted through her mind. *Where are you...come back...*

Shaking her head, she muttered, "He sent me away, lady. Besides, he thinks I'm some idiot—he thinks I am a child, some brainless little girl who doesn't know her mind."

"So prove him wrong." Sina lowered her leg and smoothed the vivid, bright cloth of her skirt down. "Although, I can tell you, he doesn't think you a child. If he did, he never would have taken you to his bed."

Spying her bag on the floor under the bed, she grabbed it and hauled it out. She pulled a pair of jeans out and tugged them on, cursing her shaking fingers. "So he enjoyed fucking me. Big deal. He got bored and sent me away."

"No, he didn't."

She jerked her head up at the new voice. It was the other Grimm—Finn. Freckle-faced, smiling Finn who used a gun to take down demons. He stood in the doorway, his hands jammed deep into his pockets, a sour look on his face.

Scowling, she said, "What?"

"He didn't send you away. I know that's what you thought, but that's not what happened."

"Finn." The woman's voice was sharp, harsh with warning.

He curled his lip at her. "Sina, bite me." He shifted his coppery eyes to Vanya and said, "Will's the one who told me I'd have to take care of you for a while, not Silence."

Vanya sagged against the bed, her hands braced on it. She blinked, tried to breathe past the knot in her throat. It didn't matter, did it? Silence hadn't once tried to come and find her.

The bed shifted. Looking up, she watched as the woman—Sina—rose. In her hand, she held something, a book, Vanya realized. She came around the bed, stopping just a few inches from Vanya, far, far too close.

"Silence has lived much of his life alone, you know," Sina said quietly. "He trusts no one. Not even me. Not completely. And I'm probably his dearest friend...his oldest lover."

Vicious jealousy ripped through Vanya. She didn't bat an eyelash as she stared at the other woman, though. Keeping her voice flat, she said, "And you're telling me this...*why*?"

"So you can try to understand." There was no anger in her voice.

And when Vanya allowed herself to look into the woman's ever-changing blue eyes, there was sympathy there. "He loves nobody—he will not allow it, because everybody he has ever loved ended up betraying him. He learned in his mortal life that he was better off alone, even if he loathed it. It's a lesson he cannot easily unlearn."

She held out the book.

Vanya looked down at it, frowned. Slowly, she took it.

"His heart already belongs to you—perhaps he hasn't told you this, but it's yours." Sina waited until Vanya looked back up at her. "If you wait much longer to answer his call, though, it will be too late. For both of you."

She turned and walked away.

"Hey...what do you mean?"

Sina paused in the door and shook her head. "I cannot tell you anymore. I see glimpses, bits and pieces of what may come. And if I share too much, it causes more problems. I've already shared too much."

Finn snorted.

She gave him a narrow look as she pushed past him.

He didn't bother moving aside.

Shaken, Vanya looked at the book she held.

At first, she wasn't sure she understood.

She traced the faded gilt of the title, frowning.

Finn ambled inside, coming to stand beside her. He craned his head, studying the title. "Huh. I always wondered."

She looked up at him.

"Wondered what?"

"Who he was." He nodded at the book. "Not all of us have a story to go along with our pasts. But many of the older ones do. I'd say that's his."

Her gut knotted as she looked back at the book.

The Man in the Iron Mask.

Her knees threatened to give out on her.

Blindly, she flung out a hand, gripped the footboard of the bed to steady herself. "Are you saying this book is based on *him*?"

"Well, loose myths anyway." Finn shrugged. "Dumas wouldn't know the real truth if it bit him. Will and the old ones, they were always very good at hiding things, rearranging things...or even pulling some pseudo-Jedi crap."

"Jedi crap?" she whispered, her voice faint.

"Yeah, you know...like *'These are not the droids you are looking for'.*" He shrugged. "But not droids. There's something of the truth in the myth that inspired this story, but you'd have to ask Silence to know the real story."

Vanya swallowed again. She'd read the book, remembered only bits and pieces. How much was true...?

A hand touched her shoulder. "You don't have time to stand there and wonder and worry right now, darlin'," Finn said softly. "Wednesday Addams out there might not want to tell you what's going on but I will."

The gravity in his voice cut through the fog in her brain.

Looking up, she met his eyes. "What is it?" she asked, suddenly terrified. "What's going on?"

"Finn—"

They looked up and saw Sina standing in the doorway. She glared at them. "You can't. She has to make the decision herself."

"She will. Once she knows what's going on," Finn said easily.

"Damn it, you young fool—" She started toward them.

He pulled Vanya away from the bed. "Don't panic, okay?"

Before she could ask, flames surrounded them. A wall of them, all around—she gasped and instinctively flung herself closer to Finn. "It's okay—they won't hurt me, and as long as you're here with me, you're good," he said. "Now listen...she won't give me much time. Silence is dying. Do you want to go to him or not?"

Vanya stared at him. "*What?*"

"That's why he hasn't come after you, I'd bet. Because he can't. He was hurt in an attack the same day the orin attacked you, although I didn't know about that until later. He was hurt pretty bad, although nothing he couldn't heal. Except he doesn't want to. He thinks he's lost you, I guess, and he's decided to give up. So...here's a question. Do you love him?"

Vanya grabbed the front of his shirt and jerked him close. "Take me to him."

"You didn't answer me," Finn said easily.

"You stupid son of a bitch," she snarled.

"Yeah. I've been called that and worse. And I'm the only one who *can* and *will* take you to him right now—he's not in a place you could ever find in time, and Will isn't coming for you. So if you want to go to him, you'll answer me, and you'll give me the truth. Do you love him?"

Starkly, Vanya stared him. "Yes." Then she tugged him closer until they stood nose to nose. "Now take me to him, you son of bitch, or I'll gut you."

The flames faded.

Sina smiled as the space beyond the flames turned out to be empty.

Perci stood behind her, her mouth gaping open.

"What in the hell...?"

"Young Finn can teleport," Sina said quietly. "He's a bit of a handful, as much a handful in this life as he was in his mortal life—he plays with fire, he teleports and he likes to shoot demons. Such a pain in the ass, that one."

"Shooting them works as well as anything else." Jack pushed past them, crouching down to study the floor. "Lucky little punk—if he'd burned up my floors, I would have kicked his ass."

"He only burns what he wants to burn," Sina said, still smiling.

Perci turned suspicious eyes on her. "You know, for somebody who was yelling at him to be quiet, you look awfully pleased."

"Well, *I* couldn't share the knowledge with her. But if it came from another source..." Sina shrugged. "I didn't see the problems arising if Finn told her. But Finn never reacted well when he was asked to do something. He always did so much better when he thought he was forbidden."

"You wanted him to tell her." Jack stood up, his arms crossed over his chest.

"Yes." Sina smiled. It was a lovely, frightening smile. She turned around and strode to the door. "You two lovebirds have a wonderful day."

She opened the door and strode through.

Perci ran to the door and jerked it open, a thousand questions still on her tongue.

But when she looked out, Sina was gone.

Vanya was going to be sick—

The moment solid ground was under her feet, she hit her knees and started to retch.

Finn touched her shoulder. "Sorry about that. I don't travel with others often and I've never figured out how to make the trip easy on them."

"Don't ever do that again," she muttered, shooting him a dirty look. She rubbed the back of her hand over her mouth, thought about saying something else, thought about hitting him, or...something. But then she noticed they weren't alone.

Will stood before them, his arms crossed over his chest, a grim look on his ageless face.

And just beyond him, on a wide, luxurious bed, lay Silence.

Although she couldn't see his face, she knew it was him. That hair, that body—she'd know it anywhere.

Despite the lurching in her gut, she shoved to her feet and started toward him. As she passed by Will, he caught her arm. She reacted by hauling off and punching him.

His head jerked back, blood fountaining from his nose.

"Feel better?" he asked, tugging a handkerchief from his pocket.

"Hey!"

Hearing a woman's voice, she turned her head, watched a slim brunette come striding toward her. Green eyes narrowed, furious, her face contorted in a scowl, the woman looked pissed.

Good—Vanya still had some rage to burn.

"Mandy, take Finn outside if you would," Will said levelly—his voice somewhat distorted.

"Like hell," she snapped.

"Now." He bit the word off, shooting her a dark look.

Finn smiled and pushed between them. "Mandy, is it? Darling, if you would be so kind, I've already had Vanya pin my ears back today—and I'm not looking forward to what she has to tell Will here. I don't think you want to listen, either..."

Vanya tuned them out, glaring at Will as they left. "Why didn't you *tell* me?"

"Why didn't you *ask*?" he replied. "Did you really think he'd leave you all on your own?"

"I wasn't alone! I had Finn with me—I thought Silence had sent him after me!" Then, abruptly, she stopped and shook her head. "It doesn't matter."

Moving around Will, she edged closer to the bed, bracing herself for what she might find. What she might see.

Her breath escaped her in a rush as she sank down on the edge of the bed. "He...he looks fine...but Finn said he's fading..."

"Silence is strong—physically. He took a grievous injury, but he heals even faster than most." Will stared at the still man on the bed. "He fades because he wishes to. Perhaps you can make him decide otherwise."

She was only barely aware of his departure, too focused on Silence's still face. Reaching out, she touched his arm.

Softly, her voice hesitant, she started to talk. Her voice trembled, but then steadied.

Sina said he'd learned that he was better off alone? She was about to show him otherwise.

The darkness had grown quiet, so quiet and complete.

When he first heard her voice, he didn't trust it.

A dream, perhaps.

Or the fitful longings of his own foolish heart.

Despite himself, though, he found himself listening. As he listened, her voice grew louder. As he listened, he found it harder to pull away.

Was she truly there...?

Hands touched him.

In the darkness, he should have hated it.

But they were her hands, stroked through his hair, taking a cloth and running it along his face, his chest. Her hands, linked with his. And her body—pressed next to his.

Silence suspected he dreamed, though. He wanted to call out to her, but if he did, and there was no answer, he knew it would shatter him. He'd chased her away, and he had no reason to hope that she'd come back now. Why would she be here?

So he clung to the dream...because it was safer. He clung to the dream because at least there he didn't have to be alone or worry that he'd wake and find her gone.

Two days and two nights passed.

Vanya talked until she was sick of the sound of her voice, until she only *wished* she could talk herself hoarse.

Thanks to the healing properties her body now possessed, though, that was almost impossible.

As twilight crept closer on the third night, she lay beside, twining her hands through his hair, her heart heavy, she said quietly, "You asked me to come back. I'm right here, Silence. Right here. So where are you?"

Exhaustion wrapped around her, claimed her. But even in her sleep, she held him close.

I'm right here.

He felt her.

Her body was warm and soft, pressed against his.

That wasn't a dream, surely.

He didn't want reach out, find her gone. Didn't want to speak and not be heard.

But the desolation in her voice made his heart ache.

Battling against the fatigue and the darkness, he forced himself to speak. It was hard, though—so hard. *"Vanya."*

He felt her stir. Felt her hand drift up to rest over his heart. And she sighed.

But she didn't speak.

He'd have to try harder...

He woke in darkness.

It was so thick and complete, for a moment, he barely realized he *had* woken.

But then he felt a soft puff of air against his chest.

With an arm that felt heavy and stiff, he shifted and reached down...and found Vanya curled around him, her head pillowed on his chest, one hand fisted just above his heart.

Sleeping.

You came back...

He closed his eyes, shaken. For a moment, he could do nothing but simply lie there and hold her as he let himself acknowledge that she was there. That she was with him. That she had come back.

Then, because the muddle of his mind was driving him mad, he forced himself to open his eyes, to look around.

Where was he?

There was something familiar...his eyes adjusted and immediately, he knew where he was. Will's cabin. Right after that, he remembered. The club. The ambush—how had they fallen for that?

Arrogance. Plain and simple. Both he and Will were both old and arrogant, convinced they could handle anything placed before them. And they'd been horribly wrong. They hadn't planned well enough, hadn't thought to look over their environment well enough before they made their attack, and they hadn't underestimated their enemy—it hadn't just been the succubae lying in wait but orin as well.

In short, they'd fucked themselves.

He'd gone down. He remembered that now, remember tasting his own blood in his throat, remembered even the look on Will's face as the other Grimm called up a power he rarely used and wiped the room clear of anything that breathed, save for Silence.

And Silence hadn't had much breath or life left in him.

Then he used another gift, the one he had for healing, holding Silence to life for so long it had damned near drained Will as well.

You won't die, damn it, Will had told him. *Not now—*

Silence had wondered if maybe it wasn't for the best.

Now he closed his eyes and buried his face in Vanya's curls. Either he'd almost made a terrible mistake or he was going to hate Will for holding him to life long enough for his body to heal the damage.

Silence didn't know which one.

Why was she here?

He stroked a hand up her narrow back and asked himself if it really mattered. Part of him didn't care. The other part, the part that desperately needed her to be there for him, because she needed him as he had come to need her, knew it mattered.

But she's already told you she loves you.

And yet he didn't know if she'd meant it...

That was what he needed to know.

First, before all else, he had to know that.

Setting his jaw, he eased out of the bed. He wore no clothes. Frowning, he glanced around for something to wear. He imagined what he had been wearing had been destroyed—bloodied and ruined.

He spied something thrown over a chair by the fireplace and he snagged it. A worn pair of loose cotton trousers. They were long enough, although he had to tie the drawstring tightly to keep them from sagging down over his arse. There was nothing else unless he wanted to raid Will's monochromatic wardrobe of white—and he had a few inches on Will, both in height and width. There was also a closet that held a female's wardrobe—certainly not an option.

The cabin, although clearly occupied, was empty now. Save for him and Vanya, who slept on deeply.

Closing his eyes, Silence waited by the fire.

When she woke, he'd have to decide.

Either he reached for what she'd offered...or he turned away from it.

He thought back over the past few centuries—thought of the loneliness, the emptiness.

He thought back farther. To his mother and father. To the man they'd allowed to take him. To the years he'd spent on his own...and then Louis and his mistress, the woman he'd one day take to wife, the sweet Françoise. She, more than Louis, had been his first true friend. He'd spent all these centuries hating Louis' treachery and not thinking of how she'd tried to stop the other man, how she'd tried to save the poor, mute boy he'd been.

Louis, the fool, had thought to use Silence for his own ends—in endless wars, in political intrigues. Françoise had seen the wrongness of it. Instead of focusing on Louis' wrongs, Silence should made himself think on what she'd risked, how she'd save his life, even that first day, how she'd befriended him.

But because he'd been hoping to find another friend in Louis, and when Louis had instead tried to use him, Silence had withdrawn. Spent all these years alone.

It wasn't how he wanted to spend the next three centuries, not even the next three decades—not even three *months*.

Not when he could spend them with Vanya.

There was a sigh behind him. Followed by a sudden cry.

He turned around just as she sat up, her hand resting on the spot where he had lain only moments earlier. Her eyes searched the room, and when they came to rest on him, it hit him like a fist to realize there were tears there. She would cry...for him.

After he'd all but rejected the love she had offered him.

She pressed her lips together, dipped her head. When she looked back at him, the tears were gone and her face was composed. "You're awake."

He started to answer but stopped himself. Instead, he just nodded.

She shifted around, swinging her legs over the edge of the bed. "You feeling okay?"

No—I hurt, I ache for you. But he didn't tell her that. Not yet. Why had she come? He needed to know that—needed to know if she had come for *him*...or out of some sense of duty.

Slowly, his hands feeling so clumsy and unsure, he signed, *Why are you here?*

Vanya looked away. A strange, bitter smile twisted her lips. "I was told you needed me. Apparently all you needed was your beauty sleep, though. I'll get out of your hair."

Frowning, he watched as she slid out of the bed, straightened clothes that were hopelessly wrinkled. She was careful never to look at him, never to so much as glance his way and how could he speak to her if she wouldn't look at him?

She started toward the door. Frustrated, he blocked her way. She still wouldn't look at him, staring at the floor, staring past his shoulder, anywhere but at him. *"If you came here for me, then why are you in such a hurry to leave?"*

She shot him a quick look, but so quick, like she didn't dare connect with his eyes. "You're awake. You're fine, obviously. And I'd left before—you weren't in any hurry to come after me before. We'll just carry on. As you were, you know." She smirked as she said it, but he caught the unsteady waver in her voice.

Stop being a coward, he told himself. As she went to go around him, he caught her arm. She jerked against him, but he didn't let go. Instead he turned, crowding her up against the door, bracing his arms on either side of her. *"Look at me,"* he ordered, lowering his face until it was on level with hers. *"Look at me, Vanya...please, love..."*

Her breath hitched in her throat. Her lashes lowered over her eyes.

But she didn't look at him.

Sighing, he dipped his head, skimmed his lips along her neck. Her scent called to him, the same way her voice did, the same way her heart did. Pressing his mouth to the curve between her neck and shoulders, he told her, *"I was coming* after you. I didn't know what I was going to do when I found you, but I wasn't just going to let you walk away, and I wasn't going to let things become some simple student-teacher thing between us. We both know it's far more than that."

She turned her head away. "Yeah, I'm the student that drops her pants the minute you look at her. I can see why you don't want to let that go," she muttered. "Too bad. I'm done with this—"

"*Don't.*" He pushed his hand into her hair, fisted it. Gently, he tugged, forcing her to meet his eyes. "*Don't make what we have into that—it's more, and we both know it.*"

"Do we?" she demanded. "*I* don't. I told you I was falling in love with you, and you pushed me away. You made me feel like I was some stupid, foolish kid and you were just humoring me. I don't know *what* we have."

"*I was wrong—you terrify me.*" Lowering his head, he pressed his brow to hers. "*You terrify me, Vanya. I've lived lifetimes—so many of them, and I've never known anybody who could terrify me the way you do. You weaken me, make me doubt...make me wonder. I've never wondered what it would be like* not *to be alone before you. It scares the life from me. And I don't handle fear well. I didn't know what you wanted from me.*"

She shook her head. Tears, once more, sparkled in her eyes. "I didn't want *anything*. All I did was tell you something—you didn't have to *do* anything."

"*I know. I figured that out.*" He pressed his lips to her eyes, kissed away the tears that had fallen. "*I pushed you away—I know that, but I did it out of fear, not because I didn't care for you.*"

Vanya swallowed. So he cared for her.

That was something...right?

But it wasn't enough.

Swallowing, she ducked out from under his arm, escaped the tempting cage of his body.

"I'm sorry it scared you. I guess I shouldn't have dumped it on you like that," she said stiffly. The knot in her throat made it almost impossible to speak, and she had to clear her throat just to manage that single sentence. Moving away from him, she stared out the window at the sprawl of mountains and trees. She had no idea where she was. No idea how to get away from here. She just hoped once she got out the door that either Will or Finn would show up—because she needed to be away from Silence, and fast.

He came up behind her, stroked his fingers down her neck. She shuddered, closed her eyes, resisted the urge to melt.

"You care for me," she said softly. "But that's not enough for me. You want to be alone. So fine—you get what you want. You can be alone. I'm not going to be some 'friend with benefits' while you decide if you want to risk *not being* alone."

Setting her jaw, setting her shoulders, she told herself to walk away. To leave.

She eased away from the window, but as she turned around, Silence continued to stand there. His hands came up, framed her face. *"I've already decided that...alone may be easier, but I will not be without you."*

His voice echoed in her mind, harsh, demanding. *Pleading...*

And even as she tried to grasp what he was telling her, his mouth covered hers. *"I love you, Vanya. I love you—and I don't want to be without you."*

She tore her mouth from his, shoved her hands between them so she could stare at him. "What?"

Tears blurred her eyes. Burned them. His hands came up and captured hers, lifting them to his mouth. He pressed a kiss to each balled up fist then guided them around his neck. Then, staring at her intently, he mouthed *"I love you"* even as he said the words into her mind. *"I love you. Now...are you still going to make me let you walk away?"*

Dumbly, she stared at him.

"No." She shoved away from him. "You're...no. This isn't happening. Damn it, you're not going to fuck with my head like this, damn it."

"Vanya—"

He caught her arm but she jerked away from him, desperate. Shaking her head, she backed away. "No. You can't tell me that I *don't* love you and then a week or so later, decide to tell me that you love me, that you want to be with me..."

She was shaking.

And he was stalking her, stalking her through the cabin as she backed away from him, his pale blue eyes intent on her face. *"Am I not allowed to fuck up? I made a mistake, and I'm sorry. I'll beg your forgiveness if you want me to—I have no pride when it comes to you."*

She was trapped now. Trapped by another window, between the huge sheet of glass and his body. As he went to his knees in front of her, she realized his image was blurring. *"I beg you, Vanya. Forgive me—I made a mistake and I'm sorry for it."*

He held her hands in his, pressing his lips to the inside of her wrists, first one then the other.

Then he lifted his head, staring at her. *"Am I to let you walk away now? You're my heart, my soul. If you don't want to be with me, I will not force you to stay. But I want you with me."*

A sob escaped her.

Tearing her hands away, she covered her face. "Shit. You're confusing me. What is this? What is this all about?"

His hands closed around her wrists and he eased them down.

"Somebody made it clear I can sit around and do nothing and lose you. I can think that you don't know your mind, although it's rather obvious you do, and have for quite some time. I can cling to my solitude. Remain alone. And you'll move on." His hand touched her face, stroking her hair back, tucking it behind her ear. "You're strong and you do not fear solitude, nor do you fear giving your heart. You'll move on and likely find a better man to give that amazing heart of yours to."

His lips skimmed along her cheekbone. "But I'm a miserable, selfish bastard. I don't want that—you're mine. I love you, damn it, and you've already given your heart to me. You're mine...unless I've already lost you."

A breath shuddered out of her as he lifted his face and stared at her. "If you tell me that you wish to walk out of here, I'll let you do it, Vanya. It's your decision. Have I already lost you?"

She closed her eyes, her heart all but shuddering in her chest. Lost her?

No.

Even if she *had* walked away, she would have still been his—her heart would have been his, whether he wanted it or not. But he wanted it...wanted *her*...

Looking back at him, she reached up and cupped his face in her hands, staring into his impossibly blue eyes. "You lose me when you decide you don't want me," she said honestly. "I thought you didn't want me, didn't need me...I was just trying to give you that."

"Then I'll never lose you because I'll always need you, always want you. Fuck, I love you."

She heard a rasping sound and barely realized he'd dragged the zipper of her jeans down. Then he caught the thick fabric, shoved it to her knees. She sagged against the window sill, her hands braced against it, staring at him as he tore at the drawstring that held up a pair of loose gray sweats.

"You..." She licked her lips. "You really mean it, right?"

He moved in, bent his knees. One hand fisted in her hair, tugging her head back. As he kissed her, she felt the rounded head of his cock nudging at her entrance. Instinctively, she tried to widen her legs, but the jeans around her knees wouldn't let her.

He pushed inside, past the resistance of her body, his body shuddering against hers. Tearing his mouth away, he gasped, mouthing her name. *"I love you—always you, only you,"* he told her.

A soft, broken cry escaped her. She arched against him, seeking to deepen the contact even as she reached up, her fingers curling his neck, digging into him, clutching him tight.

"You love me..."

"I love you. And you...you came back. You called me back..."

"Because I love you." She slanted her mouth over his and once more, struggled against the jeans trapping her legs.

Silence growled soundlessly, stooping to tear them away. She cried out as he left her, but then he was back, hooking his arms under her knees and lifting her.

He pushed inside, hard, demanding, and fast—she screamed.

"Scream again for me...let me hear it," he told her, his voice in her mind hot and smoky with approval. One hand came between them, his thumb stroking over her clit.

She whimpered, crying out.

Silence eased back, staring down at them, watching as he took her.

She watched him—staring at his face, into his eyes—

When he looked back at her, that pale, icy blue all but burned her. His mouth came back to hers, tongue and teeth nipping and tasting. *"All mine,"* he said. *"All mine, for always..."*

"I love you."

He twisted his hips, pressed against her just there—

With a cry, she climaxed around him.

And as his big body shuddered against hers, she knew he followed.

His arms, holding her tight, shook.

"You came back..." he said again. *"And I'm not letting you go."*

Vanya smiled against his damp shoulder. "I don't plan on leaving," she whispered.

They still had some things to work out, she figured. But she knew what she needed to know.

She loved him.

He loved her. And despite a lifetime of solitude, he hadn't wanted a life without her...that was enough.

About the Author

Shiloh Walker has been writing since she was a kid. She fell in love with vampires with the book *Bunnicula* and has worked her way up to the more...ah...serious works of fiction. She loves reading and writing anything paranormal, anything fantasy, and nearly every kind of romance. Once upon a time she worked as a nurse, but now she writes full time and lives with her family in the Midwest. She writes paranormal and contemporary romance, as well as romantic suspense.

You can always come home.
Second chances come a little harder.

A Forever Kind of Love
© 2011 Shiloh Walker

Chase and Zoe were the high school golden couple. Football captain, cheerleader, prom royalty. After graduation, though, Chase couldn't resist the urge to experience life outside their small town. He didn't exactly expect Zoe to wait twelve years for him, but now that he's back, he finds some small part of him hoping she did.

It's no big surprise she's married. The kick in the face is she married his best friend.

Zoe was devastated when Chase left, but she's filed those bittersweet memories under "Moved On". She loves her life, and loves her husband. She has all she needs. And Chase keeps an honorable distance.

One cold, wet, miserable day, tragedy turns Zoe's world upside down. Chase never expected her to simply fall into his arms, but a man can dream. Except his dream doesn't include the fact that this time, she's the one hitting the road…and he's the one left behind.

Warning: This story contains heartbreak, heartache and one last chance for two lovers to find each other.

Available now in ebook from Samhain Publishing.

The gods play...and mortals pay.

Bad Blood
© *2011 Lucienne Diver*

Tori Karacis's family line may trace back to a drunken liaison between the god Pan and one of the immortal gorgons. Or...maybe it's just coincidence that her glance can, literally, stop men in their tracks. While her fear of heights kept her out of the family aerobatic troupe, her extreme nosiness fits right in with her uncle's P.I. business.

Except he's disappeared on an Odyssean journey to find himself. Muddling through on her own, she's reduced to hunting (not stalking, because that would just be weird) brass-bra'd Hollywood agent Circe Holland to deliver a message...only to witness her murder by what looks like the Creature from the Black Lagoon.

Suddenly, all of her family's tall tales seem believable, especially when Apollo—*the* Apollo, who's now hiding out among humans as an adult film star—appears in her office, looking to hire her. She knows the drill: canoodling with gods never works out well for humans, but she's irresistibly drawn to him. Maybe it's her genes. Maybe not.

Given her conflicted feelings for one hot and hardened cop, it's a toss-up which will kill her quickest. The danger at her door...or her love life.

Warning: Contains pot-boiling passion between a heroine who may—or may not—be a descendent of Medusa, and a hot god and a hunky copy with the...equipment...to handle her, even on her worst bad-hair day. Beware of killer kisses, trickster gods and bearded grandmothers Who Know Everything.

Available now in ebook and print from Samhain Publishing.

It's all about the story...

Romance

HORROR

Retro ROMANCE

www.samhainpublishing.com